I0630701

PARALLAX

William Hawk

EchoPress

MICHIGAN

Published by EchoPress
Michigan, USA

Published 2018
Printed in the United States of America
ISBN: 978-0-9992887-1-9

Library of Congress Control Number: [LOCCN]

Book cover design by Whitney Scharer
Book interior design by Stacey Aaronson

This dedication is to honor those who choose to serve others over themselves.

For those that are willing to be inconvenienced for someone else's convenience.

For those that are willing to have less so others can have more.

For those that are willing to make time when they have no time to spare.

For those that love when love seems undeserved.

For those that see with their heart and not their eyes.

For those that don't want special treatment but give special treatment.

For those that will never hurt others but look for opportunities to help others.

For those that will do good no matter how much they've experienced evil.

For those that have found true joy that has nothing to do with the number of toys.

For those who look for ways to serve even if someone doesn't deserve it.

"William looked down at his host's body. This was the most challenging part of any snap, trying to figure out the body that he would be occupying for the next twenty minutes or so. His eyes landed on his host's feet, which were broad, flat and tough. The toenails were curled and yellow, the chocolate skin calloused. This man was a farmer, and if somebody had asked William to guess, he was probably a member of an ancient civilization. But the images in the parallax didn't come with captions, explanations, or even names. It was up to him to figure it all out."

CHAPTER 1

S *NAP.*

William found himself standing in the middle of a tropical field. He wore a loincloth, a long agricultural instrument in his hand.

Five hundred breaths.

The snap had started a half-second before, when William looked up at the parallax from his pod, the flickering movie-like images playing on the ceiling above his head. He'd focused on one in particular, a brown-skinned indigenous man in a green tropical field, a pyramid visible in the distance.

William had reached out and pointed his finger at the flickering image . . . and now he found himself in that indigenous man's body. He had exactly five hundred breaths to literally live in someone else's skin.

This was a "snap," also known as a tag-along. It was the term he and his team used to describe the brief space of time in which they were allowed to enter another person's body.

William was a Change Agent Level Two, typically called a CA2, as were the other four members of his team. They were trying to reach the next and highest level, a Change Agent Level Three, better known as CA3.

William felt himself take a deep breath.

Four hundred ninety-nine.

Most snaps lasted long enough for a certain event to occur. William believed that the Ancient Engineer had selected each snap for its depth of emotional experience, though that was only rumor. Nobody actually knew how the Ancient Engineer made his decisions, or did anything, nobody except for Proof.

William looked down at his host's body. This was the most challenging part of any snap, trying to figure out the body that he would be occupying for the next twenty minutes or so. His eyes landed on his host's feet, which were broad, flat and tough. The toenails were curled and yellow, the chocolate skin calloused. This man was a farmer, and if somebody had asked William to guess, he was probably a member of an ancient civilization. But the images in the parallax didn't come with captions, explanations, or even names. It was up to him to figure it all out.

He sniffed the air. It was rich, moist, loamy. Clearly, it was easy to grow crops in this type of climate.

Then William felt himself begin to move. He watched his arms throw the end of the long tool into the moist earth, turning up the soil. He felt the strain on his triceps, back and abdominal muscles. The movement felt smooth. This particular farmer had had long practice doing this exact movement.

The breeze kicked up, and his host stopped working. He stood there, feeling the breeze on his bare chest. He sipped water from an animal bladder that hung around his shoulder.

The distant brown pyramid shone close in the clear, blue sky. In the opposite direction stood a small ridge, no more than ten meters high, covered in tropical growth.

Then a sharp sound echoed from the ridge.

William felt every muscle in his host's body suddenly stiffen. This was a natural response to danger, but where had it come from?

The sound came again. It was faintly metallic. He felt his body swivel toward the danger. His eyeballs scanned the ridge as his breathing quickened.

Four hundred ten. Four hundred nine.

A light flashed on the left side of the ridge. His face quickly turned to it. In the underbrush he saw the unmistakable glint of metal.

William heard a voice yelling in an unfamiliar language. It took a moment for him to realize that it was his own voice, and it was shouting in Mayan. *I'm in the ancient Mayan civilization.* He looked behind him. A Mayan woman walked toward him from another part of the field. She was topless, a baby on her breast. His host made a gesture to stay back. She immediately stopped, but she didn't back off, just stood there staring past him.

Then he dropped to the ground behind a small mound of dirt and, through the tangle of branches, studied the commotion on the ridge. He felt his heartbeat speed up.

More flashes from the ridge. He lowered his head, then tentatively lifted it again. Watching.

Three hundred fifty-four. Three hundred fifty-three.

Then the figure came into view. It was a man wearing a

pointed metal hat. He wore another sheet of metal on his chest and strange cloth breeches on his legs. In his hand was a *halberd*, a long axe blade with a stabbing tip.

Behind him was another figure. And a third. And a fourth. All dressed in the same odd fashion.

William recognized that outfit. These were sixteenth-century Spanish soldiers. *Conquistadores.*

The Spanish soldiers carried something long and tubular. He couldn't quite make it out. They seemed to be talking among themselves. One of them turned the long tube so it was vertical to the ground, while another poured some powder into the tube and then used a long stick to push down the powder.

William's host stood up to get a better look. He felt the man's intense curiosity about the tube. Then his host approached the visitors.

The soldiers saw him and began talking excitedly among themselves. The one tamping down the powder pulled out the stick, and the others lowered the metal tube until it was horizontal and pointed the opening at William.

William knew full well what that metal tube was: a gun.

Two hundred forty-six. Two hundred forty-five.

There was more excited talking, then the tube shook and made a thunderous sound. A puff of smoke appeared at the opening. The earth next to him exploded.

William heard himself screaming as his host dropped to the ground, taking cover. He felt the man's utter confusion and panic. Then he stood up, and the curiosity flooded his body again.

A voice cried out behind William. He turned around. The

woman with the baby at her breast was shouting something at him. William felt his arm wave at her, making a gesture. It felt ambiguous.

He turned back to the soldiers. They had turned the tube vertical again, and they were dumping more powder into it. He warily approached the group, his eyes fix on the tube, half walking, then hesitating.

One hundred thirty. One hundred twenty-nine.

The Spaniards had grown agitated now, shouting at one another, pointing at William as he approached. The one dumping the powder couldn't get the stick out. He was yanking and pulling.

More shouts from behind. William turned. The woman was pointing at the strange visitors and hollering.

Then William felt something hit him in the back, between the shoulder blades. He fell to his knees, his pain receptors firing, then got back up again. On the ground lay a rock, about four inches across. The Spaniards had thrown it at him, probably out of frustration, while his back was turned.

Angry, William watched his hand pick up the rock.

Eighty-three. Eighty-two.

His arm pulled back, then windmilled forward. His hand released the rock. It cut a narrow arc through the air toward the Spaniards and glanced off one of their helmets. They began yelling. At last they pulled the stick out of the tube. As they lowered it to aim toward William, the tube exploded. One of the Spaniards stumbled backward, hands over his face, and then fell on his rear end.

William breathed a sigh of relief. They'd intended to kill

him, but the gun exploded too early. He knew that it happened frequently with early weaponry.

One of the Spaniards turned and whistled. Behind them, several more Spaniards appeared on the ridge. These men weren't wearing steel plates on their chests, and they were holding long steel knives in their hands. They ran down the slope toward William.

He felt himself hyperventilating. These Spaniards were out for blood, Mayan blood. *His* blood.

His host turned and ran backward, away from them, back toward the woman. She was retreating, too, stepping carefully with her short legs.

Sixty-seven. Sixty-six. Sixty-five.

William's host moved fluidly and carefully across the land that he'd been peacefully tilling a few minutes earlier. The squish and the squelch of the mud around his flat feet slowed him down, seeming to glom onto his heels. He imagined the same was happening to the Spaniards.

Forty-two. Forty-one.

He glanced backward. To his surprise, he saw that they were gaining on him. Their legs were longer than his. His host had probably never seen men with such long legs.

William redoubled his efforts. If he could get to the edge of the jungle, on the other side of the clearing, he could lose them.

Twenty-four. Twenty-three.

He arrived at the woman, hurried her along with his hand on her back. Her skin felt sweaty and soft. The baby had released its mouth and was starting to wail at being jostled.

A sound behind him. The Spaniards were yelling. They had gained on him. The jungle was just a few steps away.

He heard his voice urging the woman on. William presumed that this was his host's wife and child; otherwise, he would've easily gone faster.

Eleven. Ten.

The Spaniards were suddenly upon them, and William felt himself knocked to the ground. To his left, he heard a short cry, his wife had been knocked down, too. Their baby had flown a few feet away, and one of the Spaniards had grabbed the child.

William felt intense panic radiating through his body. He'd never experienced a snap this intense before.

Five. Four.

He tried to get up to reach for his baby. He felt something kick him in the ribs, and he fell over. Next to him, his wife was wailing. The Spaniards were speaking in a language he couldn't understand.

Three. Two.

One of the Spaniards stood over him and lifted the long steel knife.

"*Vaya con Dios,*" the man said.

One.

The man thrust the weapon toward William.

Snapback.

CHAPTER 2

WILLIAM'S EYES FLEW OPEN. HE WAS LYING on his back in his pod, just as he'd been five hundred breaths earlier.

He lay there, feeling himself take huge gulps of air. His body was hyperventilating, because his body thought it was still in the host's body. It wasn't, of course. His breaths were his own and free now.

The roof of the pod slid open, and he sat up and looked around the pod tank. Five pods were arranged in a circle, facing one another. They looked like futuristic coffins. William sat there, breathing, wondering what had just happened.

Next to him, a girl sat up in her pod. Her widened eyes told William that she was still agitated.

"Wow," she said.

William nodded, wiping the sweat from his face onto his sleeve. "That one almost got me, Grace."

She agreed. "That was so intense."

"Who did you snap to?"

"I was the wife with the baby."

"That was you?"

She nodded. "I think we were a couple. She had strong feelings for you." Grace took a moment to absorb it. "I've never breastfed before. It's an extraordinary sensation."

William wiped his forehead. "And I've never been one second from death before. Lucky for me my guy was hyperventilating."

On the other side of Grace, a guy sat up in the pod. He was rangy, dark-haired, with a hawklike expression. His facial features were contorted into an almost permanent sneer arranged around his beaklike nose.

"Hunter," said William, "which one were you?"

"The one that almost killed you." Hunter's face was flushed, and his eyes were filled with excitement. "That was so wild. I was right on the edge of murder." He flexed his hands and looked at them in amazement.

The other two people in the pod tank, Trina and Jeremy, lifted themselves to sitting positions as well. All five of them sat there for a moment, recovering and chatting. This was how it usually happened afterward, a few minutes chewing over what had just happened, then later a full debriefing for Proof.

A beautiful woman with almond eyes came over and undid the cuff that had been tied around William's arm. He'd forgotten it was there. "Welcome back," she said.

"Thanks, Shana." He looked up at her. Even after all these snaps—and the team had done at least twenty by now, he'd stopped keeping count—she was still a mystery. Her brown hair draped over her shoulders, and a green polyester shift draped onto her body. Her unusual face reflected a mélange of many ethnicities. A psychological wall had been erected between her and the team members, and nobody was able to breach it.

William watched her move among the team members, undoing the cuffs. Then, one by one, each of the team members climbed out of the pods and onto the floor. "It's all over your back," said Grace, looking at William from behind. He knew what she was talking about: the white goop that inevitably accumulated at the bottom of the pod during a snap. Nobody knew what it was.

William approached the third male on the team. He had pale skin, wire-rimmed glasses, and an alert manner. "Jeremy, which one were you?"

"I was tagged to one of the Spanish guys." Jeremy dropped his head. "He was just insane with greed."

"It just looked like a peaceful scene, but . . . "

"*Conquistadores* are peaceful?"

"No, just you know, the pretty field, the pyramid."

Hunter cleared his throat. "So who's ready for the debriefing?"

"I am," said Trina. She was the fifth member of the team, somewhat stouter than the others, with blonde hair and round cheeks. Her outgoing personality saved the team from taking itself too seriously. She could be considered the party girl, if there were any parties here in the quarters.

"Me too," said Grace. "This one showed me a lot."

"Like what?"

"You'll find out."

Grace smiled beguilingly as they moved out of the pod tank and down the wide corridor.

CHAPTER 3

As they entered the debriefing room, William held his hand up to his forehead, shielding his eyes from the glare.

The room was totally white. The windows, the doors, the seats, the tables, everything—a bright, blinding white. And smooth, too. The surfaces were a slick polymer.

William had never gotten used to this room. It always took him a moment to adjust to this pristine place after returning from a snap. The real world was full of browns, blacks, greens and blues, a thousand different textures, a million different sounds and smells, but not here. All those elements had been antiseptically removed from this room.

But this wasn't the real world. This was the debriefing room.

The other members of the team walked in after him. Trina bounced happily in her shoes. Grace moved with her customary, well, grace. Hunter loped like a wolf, and behind him Jeremy moved quietly, his eyes taking everything in. They moved comfortably because they'd all done this many times before. They knew how the routine went.

The room was littered with chairs, sculpted and swooping modernist pieces. William took a seat in his customary one. They'd all quickly settled into habits, preferring certain seats.

He looked down at the cup in the holder in the armrest of the chair. It was already full of the odd liquid that they found here following every snap. It looked almost like tea, but not quite. He lifted the cup to his lips. Its flavor reminded him of something, but exactly what was always just out of reach. He suspected that it served some purpose other than refreshment.

Grace sat down next to him, Trina on the other side. They seemed to see that he was still shaken by the experience.

A whirlwind of white passed through the room, looking like a tornado of sheets. When it stopped sidewinding, a man stood before them, skin pale like a dove, his green eyes intelligent and playful and stern all at once. He carried a fairly large muscular frame. William thought he bore a passing resemblance to a construction worker.

This was Proof. He was the leader of the team, the coach, the counselor, the disciplinarian. His was the first face that William saw when he arrived, and most likely it would be the last one he saw before he departed.

"What do you think of the entrance? Too much?"

"You looked like a spastic phantom," cracked Hunter.

William was surprised when he first arrived here. He'd been called up, with the four others, from the realm of Menoram. It was where souls waited for assignment. He didn't remember much about it, except that it was kind of like living inside an energy field, waiting for an unknown destiny, and with awareness but still being unaware.

Here, with this team, however, he had the opportunity to advance himself. He had free will.

Proof walked through the room, touching each of them on the shoulder, saying their names. It was his little ritual. "Where did you go in this tag-along?"

He still used the term tag-along, meaning that the team tagged along emotionally with their hosts. Most everybody else agreed that the term *snaps* was better, since they were so short.

"We think it was Ancient Maya," said Grace. "William and I were indigenous, the others were Spanish soldiers."

"Ah, that one," said Proof. "I did that one once. What did you think?"

"Well," said Trina, "William's host almost got killed."

"By mine," said Hunter.

"He probably did get killed," said Jeremy, "but only after the snapback."

Proof leaned back and smiled. "We used to call those photo finishes. Everybody encounters them. It's a good learning experience."

William looked down at his cup. The strange tea had refilled itself. No matter how many times they came to the debriefing room, he would never get tired of seeing that happen.

Then he raised his hand. "Proof? What would've happened if I'd been in the host when he was killed?"

"It's hard to say exactly," admitted Proof. "We've focused on making more meaningful experiences that would advance you."

"Would I be trapped forever?"

He shrugged. "You would have to ask the Ancient Engineer."

The Ancient Engineer. Nobody'd seen him, and his name carried mythic status, but everyone knew one thing about him: The Ancient Engineer had apparently designed everything. The pods, the station, the tag-along techniques, even the Change Agent hierarchy. All of it had been his design, and perhaps even much more.

William stared daggers at Hunter. "Is it possible to stop a host from killing someone?"

Proof nodded, "Of course, but . . . "

Hunter finished his thought, staring at William. "But we're not supposed to interfere with the movements, feelings or thoughts of the hosts. It was in training."

"But we just said that death is uncharted."

"Hold on," said Grace, putting her hands out toward both of them. "William, he didn't know that you were in that host body. And you didn't know that he was in his. And neither of you can affect the actions of the hosts anyways, so why bother arguing?"

"We're all just guessing who is who in a snap," added Trina.

Proof looked around. He and Jeremy made eye contact. It looked as though Jeremy had something to say.

"What is it, Jeremy?"

"I think there's a way to communicate while we're in the snap," he said.

Proof clapped his hands, then pointed at him. "Everybody, Jeremy is making a breakthrough."

The other four, who had been talking animatedly, suddenly shut up. They turned toward Jeremy.

"Say it again, Jeremy," said Proof.

"I think we, the five of us, can communicate with one another in a snap," he said.

"How?" said Trina.

"I don't know how exactly, but I could somehow feel you, Grace," he said. "I could almost hear you, too."

Proof snapped his fingers. The room went dark, and a spotlight landed on Jeremy.

"Jeremy just took another step up the chain," said Proof.

The others clapped. The lights went back up, and Hunter looked agitated. "Why does it happen to him? Why not me?"

"Because he's improving his range of experience, and therefore his range of empathy. We're all part of the same energy." Proof spread his hands out. "People, people, what is with this bickering? You've been selected by the Ancient Engineer, *the Ancient Engineer himself*, to elevate yourselves. Do it! All of you have the ability to rise to CA3. That is why you're here! Cooperate! Learn from one another!"

William now understood that this was referring to the Change Agent designation. A CA1 (Change Agent Level One) was a normal human on earth, which is where all of them had started out. A CA2 was granted extra powers of perception and intuition, sometimes even telekinetic powers. A CA3 existed at the top of the scale and was granted nearly superhuman abilities. That's where they were all trying to get, but they had to do it as a team. If one person couldn't advance, *nobody* would make it. Proof had explained that the

Ancient Engineer found that this method improved the efficiency of the advancement. It was the same principle that made teachers assign group projects to high school students.

The only problem, however, was that there was always one person who didn't contribute to group projects.

Meanwhile, they'd learned recently that there was another level of Change Agent: a CA0. This was a fallen Change Agent, one who had reached the top of the great chain of understanding, but who had begun to use the awareness for evil. Proof had reluctantly discussed it. It was clear that he preferred to focus on more positive matters.

In any event, everyone on this team had already achieved CA2. William, Grace, Jeremy, Trina, even Hunter, despite the fact that he'd begun causing trouble. He was what they called a rotten apple.

And William fervently hoped that he wouldn't spoil the bunch.

"Now it's time to name that emotion," said Proof. This was how they ended every debriefing. Each person had to name an emotion that he or she had experienced either for the first time or to a greater degree than ever before. "Trina?"

"Boredom," she said.

"Interesting," Proof replied. "That was the first time you felt bored in a tag-along?"

She nodded. "I was tagged to this Spaniard soldier at the back of the group. He was just guiding a pack mule." She nodded toward William and Hunter. "I never even saw the fight that they've been talking about."

"But what did you learn from that experience?"

She thought about it. "Maybe that there's dignity in work. This guy was patiently doing his job."

Proof waved a device up and down her body. It looked like a thin wand, about the length of a human hand. The device beeped approvingly. "The spectrometer says yes."

William tried not to smile. Proof had earned his name for a very good reason. It's what he demanded after every snap. He was quantifying the emotional and spiritual progress of each member of the team, but exactly *how* these things were quantified was never explained. William secretly hoped that they would meet the Ancient Engineer to get more concrete explanations.

"Jeremy?" said Proof.

"I was with the Spanish team, too," he said. "I felt trapped."

"Like you weren't in charge of your own destiny?"

"Exactly. I was tagged to a foot soldier who didn't even want to be there."

"How did it make you feel?"

"Awful." Jeremy looked around. "Free will is everything, people. I mean it."

Proof waved the spectrometer up and down the young man. *Beep.*

"Good," he said. Then he turned to William. "And you?"

William felt a stirring of anxiety in his stomach. "Well, I definitely found a new emotion tonight."

"What is it?"

"Fear. I felt total and complete fear."

"Of what?"

"You heard the story. Of death."

Proof nodded. He waved the spectrometer across William. It beeped approvingly.

Then he turned to Hunter. "Let's hear it, Hunter."

His dark eyes fixed on Proof. "Bloodlust."

"You wanted to kill somebody?"

"Like I've never experienced."

Proof tilted his head ever so slightly. "And you liked it?"

"No." Hunter waited a beat. "I *loved* it."

Proof stood there, regarding him for a moment. Then he waved the spectrometer, and it beeped.

"Mine was motherly love," said Grace. "I had a baby on my breast."

"Strong stuff, isn't it?" said Proof, turning toward her. "I tagged a new mother once. It gives you a whole new perspective." He waved the device, and it beeped.

"Congratulations," he said, "you've all made advancements today."

Grace's hand shot up. "So when do we get to see how close we are to CA3?"

"Those algorithms are created and guarded by the Ancient Engineer. Remember, what do we know about the Ancient Engineer?"

In unison, the group said, "He loves us, and he wants us to succeed."

Proof reclined in his seat. "Tomorrow, it's Grace's turn to select the parallax. That's all for now everybody."

The lights dimmed in the room. William looked down at his cup. It was empty. He and the other team members stood up one by one.

"Hey Grace," said Hunter.

"What?"

"Pick a good one tomorrow. Like a war or something. I want to feel what it's like to kill somebody."

Hunter moved ahead down the hall, and Grace looked back at William with alarm in her eyes.

CHAPTER 4

THAT EVENING, THE TEAM MEMBERS WERE free to do as they pleased. William would typically find a book, watch a video, or sometimes huddle with Jeremy in a distant corner and discuss deep thoughts. Life and love, lives and loves, the nature of existence. They'd had some pretty heavy talks, and the later it got, the heavier the conversation grew.

Tonight, however, William was feeling more social, so he found himself wandering into the recreation room. Free to use for everybody, it was lined with books on the walls and had board games, tables and comfortable recliners.

He saw Trina sitting on a sofa, staring at one of the lime-green walls.

"What are you doing?" said William.

"Being bored." She thought about it. "Since I'm always bored in the snaps, I thought I would try to do it on purpose. It's not that bad."

Jeremy lay in one of the recliners, reading a book called *The Psychology of Psychology*.

Nearby, Grace chucked a small bit of paper at him. Jeremy looked up. "What?"

"That," she said, "looks like the most redundant book ever."

"I knew you were going to say that."

"How?"

"Because this is a book on psychology, and people are predictable."

"Shut up."

"See, I knew you were going to say that, too."

William shook his head, bemused. Sometimes the conversation got kind of weird here. In the evenings, it felt like a graduate school dorm room bull session.

William looked at Grace. "Don't you have anything better to do?"

She shrugged. He already knew that would be the answer. It was well known that she tended not to do any preparation at night, which made the others jealous, because she was probably the most advanced of the group. Proof hadn't come right out and said it, but everybody could tell that she was his favorite. He talked to her with more respect.

"What would you like me to be doing?" she said.

"You could be doing anything. Watching video."

"I'll leave that to Hunter."

"Ten bucks says he's in the monitor room," said Trina.

"Nobody will take that bet," said William.

"What's he watching this time?" said Trina.

"Twentieth-century snuff films," said Jeremy from behind his book. "That's his new pastime."

They all fell quiet. The challenge, as laid out by Proof, was to elevate oneself above the temporal, the basic, the common, and to get in touch with the invisible but essential strings that connect all creatures. The team's common goal, of course, was to achieve CA3 status, but *they had to do it as a group*. William couldn't see how watching videos of entrails and horrific mutilations would elevate one's soul. In fact, he was worried about Hunter's impact on the team. He seemed to be going in the opposite direction. If anybody was going to hold them back, it would be Hunter.

"How do you know?" said Grace.

Jeremy looked up. "I could hear him behind the door. The audio was full of screams. And Hunter was, like, cackling."

William rolled his eyes. "You know what, I'm going to go pull him out of there."

Grace caught him by the arm. "I wouldn't try. Trina tried it a few days ago, and he got really angry."

"He can be angry," said William, "but he's going to listen to me."

"I wouldn't be too sure about that," said Grace.

William left the recreation room and headed to the monitor room. He felt a deep anger stirring inside, a sense of injustice. The thick white door was closed, and the red light indicated that it was locked.

He walked up to the door and pounded on it with the heel of his palm. "Hunter, open up! We got a problem out here! Hurry up, I need you!"

"Go away," said a muffled voice inside. The tiny sounds of screams were echoing out of the monitors.

"I'm serious, buddy," William said. "Proof told us that we've got a problem with the parallax projectors."

He heard the tiny screams inside the room stop. He heard a chair slide across the floor.

Then the door swung open. Hunter stood there, a full four inches taller than William, his face flushed and angry.

"That's bullshit," he hissed.

William put on his best casual face. "Maybe, maybe not. How are things going, buddy? We haven't seen much of you." He peered over Hunter's shoulder. The monitor showed a live bird being ripped to pieces, the bloody entrails strewn across a patch of dirt. "Whatcha watching?"

"Something stimulating," he growled.

"I bet that's the truth."

Hunter got that narrow, irritated look on his face. "So really there's no problem with the parallax projectors?"

"Nah," said William, "I was just playing with you. But I do have a bigger concern." He stepped forward, lowered his voice. "We're all in this together. You know that, right?"

"Yes."

"If you don't succeed, then we don't succeed. And then we all go right back to Menoram. You're okay with that?"

"William, you're not my mentor. Besides, I'm probably more advanced than you."

William tried to hide a smile. Hunter was seeing this as a competition. "Are you sure about that?"

"Yes."

"My friend, I'm not the one watching animal mutilation for fun." He put his hand on Hunter's shoulder. "Come out to the rec room."

Hunter swiped William's hand off his shoulder. "Just leave me alone."

But William wasn't ready to drop the confrontation.

"Can I ask a question?"

"You can ask. I might not answer."

"Are you a good guy?"

Hunter looked at him but didn't say anything. Then he stepped backward. The door slid shut, and the red light blinked on. Locked. William heard the chair scrape on the floor. Tiny screams began to sound again.

William sighed and turned and went the other way down the hallway. Even though he was unsuccessful, he'd tried, and Hunter was a tough nut to crack.

CHAPTER 5

THE NEXT MORNING, THE FIVE MEMBERS OF the team ate breakfast in the galley. On William's plate was a single poached egg, a strip of bacon, a mess of fried potatoes, and some greens. He always needed a big meal in the morning. Jeremy had followed his lead and begun asking for the same, while Trina dug into a vegetarian bowl. Hunter was busy defiling a piece of bloody steak, the same thing he ate every morning. Grace, meanwhile, was picking at a small bowl of yogurt with fruit. She never seemed to feel like eating much first thing in the morning, even though she'd been advised to have something in her stomach before the morning snap.

"How many snaps do you think we're going to do before we reach CA3 status?" said William.

"They won't say," replied Hunter.

"I hope they give us as many as we need," Grace said. "I mean, I feel like we're advancing. Hopefully, we are."

"Jeremy definitely did yesterday," said Trina, "but I'm spinning my wheels."

"Just be patient," said Jeremy.

"It's frustrating," said Trina. "I don't feel it like you guys do. We go into these snaps, and you guys come back talking all about breastfeeding and the fear of death, and you're all so excited. Me, I just feel bored. Every time. And I don't know what to do about that."

"Proof understood yesterday," said William.

"And the spectrometer doesn't lie," added Jeremy.

Trina pushed back from the table. "I just don't know if this is going to end well. And I don't want to hold back the team."

She left the galley. The others continued eating their breakfast in silence, but Grace got to her feet. "I'm going to keep her company. I'll see you guys there shortly."

"It's your choice today," he said, "so we're all waiting on you."

William arrived at the pod tank a few minutes later. Usually, Grace arrived first, but this morning he entered before the others.

When he arrived, Shana was waiting with the sensor, a small double-tined fork. William turned his arm out, and she pricked his skin quickly. It hurt the first time, but he'd gotten used to the swift pain. Proof explained the sensor once, saying that it was for research purposes. Nobody knew exactly what type of research he meant, not exactly.

William went over to his pod. It was his in the same sense that a chair was yours in a classroom; everybody tended to choose the same pod every day, even though they were all the same. It looked like a long coffin. Shana had cleaned out the white goop, as she did every night.

"Shana, what is that white stuff that always appears in our pod?"

"We pour it inside as soon as you go into the tag-along," she replied "It serves as a kind of spiritual conductor. It makes the experience a little crisper."

"Proof never told us about that."

"Maybe nobody ever asked."

William climbed into his pod. It was made of some type of polymer that was slightly spongy, like the bottom of a playground mat. It was always cool to the touch.

"I have another question," he said.

"Okay."

"Are we ever going to meet the Ancient Engineer?"

Shana was matter-of-fact. "It depends entirely upon him. And you. Lie back please."

William lay down in the pod, feeling the back of his head come to a rest against the polymer. It was comfortable here, like a firm but slightly giving mattress. A person could comfortably lie here all day without falling asleep.

Shana came over with the armband and affixed it to his right bicep. It featured a digital readout. William didn't need to look down to know what it was showing, a continually changing series of biometric readings, including heart rate, internal temperature, and other core body processes.

"How many snaps have you done?" said William.

"You have a lot of questions today," came her reply. "But the answer is a few hundred."

"So you should be a CA3 by now."

"No, I'm not," she said.

"Why not?"

"It's a long story," she said. "Close your eyes and get ready."

William obediently shut his eyes, and she slid the top of the pod over his body. Now he was encased entirely in a pure white polymer pod. His eyes tracked the soft blue light that ran around the edges of the pod, casting a pleasing glow. He watched as the light slowly moved through the entire chromatic spectrum: indigo, violet, red, orange, yellow, green, and back to blue. He felt hypnotized.

From outside came the sound of footsteps as the others arrived and climbed into their pods. Then he heard the soft sounds of the lids being closed.

At last, the colored lights dimmed, and through the frosted translucent case, William could see the various images of the parallax begin flickering on the ceiling. He turned his head. In the pod next to his, Grace sat with the top open, looking at the choices. This was customary; William had done the same yesterday.

He saw her arm lift toward the ceiling and point. He wondered which one she chose. They all had their own prejudices. Trina liked tropical sites; Jeremy favored darker, moodier locations; while Hunter was flatout unpredictable. William wasn't quite sure about his own preferences. Mostly he was just interested in meeting new people. He was just thankful to have been given the opportunity to be here.

Then the pod fell away, and William felt himself falling away, down, down, through a long tunnel, bits of light flashing past him.

CHAPTER 6

FIVE HUNDRED BREATHS.

William was astride a horse hurtling across an open range. He wore a felt coat with long sleeves that covered his arms and hands. His elbows were loose, and his body was relaxed on the animal's broad back. The horse had a long shaggy mane.

The air was sharp and clean, the grass green and long. Overhead, the sky shone an intense shade of brilliant blue that he'd never seen before. The sound of the horse galloping on the ground beat a tattoo under the sound of the wind whistling past his ears.

William turned his head. Next to him pounded another horse. It had a larger head, a shaggier coat, and stubbier legs than he had expected to see. He guessed that was probably to help the animal survive winters.

The rider, like William, wore a traditional coat that was as blue as the sky overhead and a loose ankle-length robe with a high collar that was buttoned from the left over to the right shoulder. William felt the lining inside his own coat and guessed that it was probably made of sheepskin or fox. Underneath his coat were heavy pants tucked into boots, which were curved up to tiny points. Lastly, around his waist was a sash, and William could feel a knife riding there.

The other rider turned and looked at William with hard, cruel eyes. His face seemed vaguely Asian, but not Vietnamese or Cambodian or Japanese. The face was a lighter shade and wide with higher cheekbones.

William suddenly knew where he was.

In Mongolia.

His host turned around, and William got a glimpse of the size of the group he was travelling with. Behind him were a thousand riders on horseback, all trampling across the plain. A massive cloud of brown dust rose into the air behind the group.

He was part of an enormous Mongolian horseback army.

Four hundred eleven. Four hundred ten.

Then William saw something else that surprised him.

About a hundred feet behind him, a globe seemed to float around one rider's head. It looked like a helmet of light, an aura or a bubble, much like the ones that Christian painters of old used to depict holy people. This particular one was a pale blue.

He remembered the word. It was a *nimbus*, and he got a strong sense that this rider was Jeremy's host. He couldn't say how he knew. It was just an intuitive thing. He knew that was Jeremy the same way he knew that he liked bacon and eggs.

He looked to the other side. Another rider had drawn up alongside his horse, the animals' hoofbeats echoing one another. This soldier had an orange nimbus, and William's intuition told him that this was Grace's host.

Scanning the pack of riders, William saw the other two nimbi. A hundred meters back bobbed a third one, a yellow one; he knew it was Trina. The fourth was on a distant horseman, separated from the rest of the pack, and it was black, so black that it nearly obscured the rider's face. That was definitely Hunter. As William watched, Hunter's host swung his butt out over the side of his horse and dropped two steaming turds on the ground. The horse never stopped running.

That was definitely Hunter's behavior. William wondered if he'd found a way to manipulate his host's behavior, or if Mongolian horsemen always acted that disgusting. It was entirely possible that Mongolians crapped off the sides of their horses for fun.

They rode for a few more minutes, and William marveled at the wildlife on the hillside. Little ground animals scurried into their dens as foxes chased after prey. Swans floated down the streams that crossed the plains. Ravens swept across the landscape, while hawks perched on rocks, waiting for a meal.

On a nearby horse, another rider lifted an arm, and William felt his host tugging the horse's head to the left. About fifty others did likewise, and soon he realized that this was a division of the army, and that they were headed somewhere in particular.

Three hundred thirty-eight. Three hundred thirty-seven.

In the distance, tucked into the foothills, a series of small circular structures appeared. William rode up to one, stopped the horse, and hopped off. Twenty other riders arrived, one by one, including the other members of William's team. The nimbi made them easy to spot.

The soldiers laced their horses together by tying the reins to a common line, then turned toward the structure. William recognized it as a *ger*, more commonly known as a yurt. It was the traditional shelter for Mongolians who lived in the rural areas.

William felt himself talking to another soldier about the rain clouds on the horizon. Then they were chatting about the likelihood of finding alcohol or a pretty young girl in the *ger*. This conversation wasn't particularly enlightening. As far as William knew, soldiers had been seeking food and sex for as long as there were soldiers.

William's host gazed at the structure. The wooden framework appeared to be sturdy. A layer of felt made from animal hair covered the roof and sides. Sturdy ropes helped hold the felt in place, and huge rocks anchored it all in place when the wind blew, which was probably often. A wooden door had been placed on the side facing southeast.

One of the soldiers cupped his hands and shouted at the *ger*. A dog started barking. A minute later, a man came out through the doorway. Dressed in shabby clothing, he was probably a herder. Next to him stood a young boy, not more than seven years old. The child ran to the dog and sat down on its head. The dog stopped barking.

The soldier and the man exchanged greetings. Then the man welcomed the soldiers to enter his ger, one at a time, to receive some airag, the fermented horse milk that was the universal Mongolian welcome beverage.

Two hundred forty-five. Two hundred forty-four.

William felt himself walk across the grass toward the ger. The herder greeted him warmly, with a broad smile and open gestures. The door was painted a bright red.

He entered the house, realizing that his hand was on the knife in his sash. Just in case. He sensed from the host that using it wasn't unheard of.

Inside, double poles with a wooden ring at the top had been placed in the center of the circular home. Rafters were inserted into the ring, and long orange poles connected the ring with the top of the walls, which were hung with patterned fabric curtains. There were no windows except for an open flap at the top, allowing for ventilation.

William took in the rest of the *ger*. The marriage bed stood opposite the entrance, holding cushions for sitting and quilts and clothing. A low wooden stool in front of the bed indicated the guest's place of honor, facing the entrance. A chest with a Buddha altar was nearby, painted orange, which seemed to be a good luck color. Saddles and hunting gear were nearby, on the left side of the ger, protected by the sky god. A single carpet had been thrown over the dirt floor.

In the center of the floor was the man's wife, who crouched over a large bag that was tied to a pole, whirling the bag. William felt his host smile. This must be the *airag*.

One hundred seventy-two. One hundred seventy-one.

Three other soldiers entered the ger, and William joined them in taking seats on the low stools. One of them was Hunter, the black nimbus so obvious to William that he was surprised nobody commented on it. The woman opened the bag and dumped the liquid into a wooden bowl and handed it to William. He took it in his right hand, flicked three drops to the sky, then inhaled. It smelled milky and acidic and bitter and floral all at once. Then William felt himself take a sip. It was a strange liquid, sour and alcoholic, but his host enjoyed the flavor.

The woman passed around a hard-dried curd that looked like a biscuit. They all took turns gnawing at it. William thought it was decent. He'd learned in these snaps that what passed for food depended greatly upon region, era and class status.

Eighty-four. Eighty-three.

Across the hut, Hunter's host suddenly reached over and picked up one of the saddles, threw it over his shoulder, and stood up. He started to leave the ger, but the owner stopped him at the door. They got into a heated conversation, with both of them gesturing to the saddle and the horses outside. The man tried to take the saddle from Hunter's shoulder. Hunter became upset, the nimbus grew even darker, and he pulled his arm back as if to strike the man.

The atmosphere grew thick with tension.

Fifty-two. Fifty-one.

The other soldiers leapt to their feet and restrained Hunter. He immediately changed, the nimbus grew less dark, his body relaxed, and he lowered his arm. He sat down at his stool again.

Everybody relaxed. William's host let out a giant sigh of relief. William, meanwhile, had a sneaking suspicion about what had just happened.

Hunter had made his host try to steal the saddle.

Thirty-seven. Thirty-six.

The owner left the hut and returned carrying what looked like a bloated, furry ball. It was blackened and burnt and disgusting. The charred smell invaded William's host's nostrils. He guessed that it had once been a large prairie rodent, maybe a marmot.

The man put the thing on a wooden tray in the middle of the room, and then slit it open with a knife. Hot coals and nearly raw animal entrails spilled out of the animal's belly and onto the tray. Using the knife, he cut the entrails into pieces, one by one.

As he did so, William felt his host's stomach rumble. William had committed to this experience, but part of him hoped that the snap would finish. Quickly. Raw marmot intestine wasn't his idea of enlightenment.

Sixteen. Fifteen.

The man speared a chunk of pink animal intestine on his knife and handed it to a soldier. Then he did the same to another, and to another. Then to Hunter. William watched them chewing contentedly, small grunts of pleasure coming from their mouths.

Nine. Eight.

Finally, the man speared a chunk of the delicacy and handed it to William, a big open smile on his face. The man was nothing if not hospitable. William watched his fingers take the meat.

Four. Three.

William watched himself lift the raw innards to his mouth.

Two.

The intestine touched his tongue.

One.

The flavor of raw excrement filled his mouth.

Snapback.

CHAPTER 7

IN THE POD, WILLIAM SNAPPED AWAKE, the horrendous taste still in his mouth. He turned his head and spit into the white goop that had appeared at the bottom of the pod tank, as usual.

He heard Shana moving around outside, opening each of the pods.

At last, his own slid open. Shana unfixed the armband and offered him her hand. William ignored it, preferring to pull himself out.

Hitting the floor, William's feet felt strangely heavy. He'd noticed that his reaction to each snap was different. Sometimes he felt giddy, sometimes he felt sad, sometimes he felt ineffable awe.

This time, he felt both excitement and a deep sense of unease, and he knew the reason for both.

"How was it?" Shana asked.

"I ate raw animal turd," he replied.

Surprise registered on her face. "For real? I hate it when that happens."

"Totally putrid. It was *awful.*"

"Once I went to a snap in Borneo that turned into a cannibal family picnic." Shana shook her head at the memory of it. "I will never forget that."

Around them, the others were stepping out of the pods. Every member of the team experienced each snap differently, depending on many factors, particularly the type of host they were assigned to. At the moment, Trina looked frightened, while Jeremy just seemed tired. After all, not every snap was created equal. Some would be more intense experiences than others. It was a numbers game, in a sense. Proof had explained that they were simply seeking individual breakthroughs. William's breakthrough had arrived today. He was able to see the nimbi as clear as day.

And he'd also seen something else.

He watched Hunter climb out of his pod. His teammate wore an artificially relaxed look on his face, as though he knew he'd just gotten away with something.

When he noticed William standing nearby, he ambled over casually. "Mongols, man! Pretty wild, huh? I always wondered what it was like to be part of Genghis Khan's army."

"I figured that was where we were," said William.

"Yeah, it definitely was. My host kept thinking about him."

"Mine didn't." William decided to venture a small comment. "Hey, did your host want to steal that saddle?"

Hunter's narrow eyes searched William's. "How did you know my host tried to steal a saddle?"

"You'll find out."

Hunter made a lateral movement with his hand as though wiping things clean. "I had nothing to do with that, man. We don't always tag-along with the nicest people in the world."

With that, a vicious wink fluttered briefly at the corner of his eye. Than Hunter walked away, and William watched him go. He felt suspicion in nearly every inch of his being.

Hunter had just lied to him.

Later, in the debriefing room, William sipped the strange tea beverage and watched as Proof went around the room, eliciting responses.

"I felt terror," said Grace.

"Why?"

"My host tried to steal a girl, and her father caught him."

"What happened?"

She dropped her head. "There was a fight. He beat me."

Proof put a hand on her shoulder. "Remember, it was just a tag-along. You were a visitor to their time and place."

"I know, I know. It's just, we've discussed this before, the whole violence thing."

"Violence is a part of life," said Hunter.

"I'm not talking about killing animals for food," Grace said. "I'm talking about *unnecessary* violence."

"Killing animals is unnecessary," said Trina.

"You're a vegetarian," said Hunter.

"So what?" she shot back.

"Shana's not a vegetarian because she loves animals," said Jeremy. "She's a vegetarian because she hates plants."

"Will you shut up," she said, laughing.

"Anyways," said Proof, trying to calm them down, "let's pick up this topic later tonight. I'd like to move to William's experience."

William cleared his throat and shifted in his seat. "Well, this was an interesting one, because for the first time, I could identify everybody."

Proof looked confused. "Who is everybody?"

"The five of us."

"How?"

William calmly explained how he was able to see nimbi around everybody's heads. He described the colors, the textures, the translucence. Proof's eyes grew wide, and he faced William square on.

"You've just made a huge step forward," he said.

"Have I reached CA3?"

A hush from the others as they waited for his response. "Well, let's not go too far. In the meantime, congratulations."

He congratulated William with a handshake. The others breathed out audibly, and William could tell that they'd been concerned about an imbalance on the team. "Proof, there's something else I've been thinking about."

"Tell me."

William summoned all his courage. He was about to open a Pandora's box, and once open, it couldn't be closed. "I'm concerned about Hunter."

Across the room, Hunter had been slouching in his seat, picking his fingernail. At the mention of his name, however, he shot up rigid and straight. "What did I do to you?" he spat.

Proof's face grew serious. He crossed his arms and backed

away from the group a few steps. "Let's hear your concern."

The others fell silent. William felt himself growing nervous, but he'd committed to this confrontation. "You haven't done anything to me. However, I watched your host try to steal a saddle inside the ger."

Hunter grew annoyed. "And I already told you that I couldn't control him."

"But I was reading about Mongolian culture today," said William, "and that kind of crime is unheard of. To steal something from a home where you're a guest just doesn't happen, not at any point in history. These are the most generous people on earth."

Hunter shrugged. "So my host was a bad guy."

"But he acted oddly. Before the theft, he was normal. Then suddenly he picked up this expensive saddle and tried to walk out of someone's home with it. And the others had to restrain him. Then afterward, he sat down like nothing had happened."

"I don't understand what you're saying," said Jeremy.

Trina interrupted. "He's saying that Hunter is influencing his host's behavior."

Hunter's face had turned into a strange, tortured caricature of pain. His voice came out tight and angry. "I would *never* influence a host to do anything. I don't even know *how* to influence a host."

"Are you sure about that?" said William.

Hunter spread his arms out wide, and his voice nearly broke from the stress. "Of course I'm sure! I'm not hiding anything from you!"

The others looked to William, who looked to Proof. The leader was stroking his chin thoughtfully. Nobody could read him.

"It's true," said Proof, "that not all the people you tag-along with will be sterling characters. Let's give Hunter the benefit of the doubt on this one." Then to Hunter he said, "We'll talk later."

Hunter slumped back in his seat, angry, defensive.

Proof turned back to the rest of the team. "So what do we know about the Ancient Engineer?"

In unison, the group said, "He loves us, and he wants us to succeed."

Proof reclined in his seat. "Jeremy, it's your turn tomorrow. Have a good one, everybody."

The lights dimmed. Hunter stood up and quickly ran out of the room. By the time the other four team members had reached the corridor, the renegade was already in his room, locking the door behind him.

CHAPTER 8

WILLIAM SAW THE STEAM ON THE frosted glass door of the steam room, and he knew full well who was sitting inside.

Hunter was still in his room, Jeremy and Trina were having a game of cards. It was Grace.

Taking a deep breath, he ran to his room, changed into his swimsuit, then ran back. He yanked open the door.

"William!" she said.

He stepped backward. "Grace? I'm sorry, do you want me to come back?"

"No, just wait!"

His heart soared at that. *She didn't want him to leave.* He caught sight of her figure vaguely through the mist. She seemed to be fastening something around her torso. "No, it's okay now, come in."

Hesitantly, he stepped into the steam room and closed the door behind him. He sat down on the opposite end of the wooden bench from Grace.

"There's a do-not-disturb sign you can hang out there," he said.

"I didn't know that," she said.

"Yes. Unless you wanted to be disturbed."

"Not necessarily," she replied. The steam had dissipated slightly, and he could see her crossing her arms over her body. William sat there, breathing in the wet moisture, feeling the beads of water form in the hollow space of his sternum. He puffed up his chest to make himself look bigger, just in case she was watching him through the hot mist.

Grace finally broke the silence. "So did you *really* see nimbi around our heads today?"

"Yep," said William. "Yours was orange."

"Maybe those old religious painters had powers to see nimbi too."

William nodded. That thought had occurred to him. Then he felt the anger rising up again. "The thing about Hunter, though, I wasn't lying, or starting crap. I *know* he was influencing his host."

"How do you know?"

"That's the thing, Grace, it was just intuitive. I can't explain it any better than the fact that I could see him acting through the Mongolian soldier. I mean, I even watched him take a dump off the side of his horse. Without stopping!"

Grace laughed, then turned her body toward him. "That sounds like something the Mongol horde probably did regularly."

"But in the tent, I swear, it was Hunter acting."

"I'm not doubting you, William. Did you notice that nobody defended him in the debriefing?"

"Yeah."

"If that's true, then the real problem is that he isn't telling us everything he knows how to do."

William rubbed his forehead. "I know."

"And if that's true, then what happens next? Does he take advantage of us somehow? Either here, or in a snap?"

Grace shrugged. "I don't know. Only the Ancient Engineer would be able to tell you that."

The room had cooled. Grace went over to the heating stones and dumped more water on them. A cloud of steam rose from the stones, filling the room. William felt the heat flushing his cheeks once more, though it could've just as easily come from sitting so close to Grace. She was attractive, both in body and in spirit, and William's mind was racing through possible romantic scenarios, all ludicrous. She could trip and fall into his pod.

A passion building in his chest made him decide to go for broke. With no prompting, William reached out his hand and placed it on Grace's hand. She looked at him, and he looked back at her. He admired the beads of water condensing on the tip of her nose. His eyes glanced down at the soft skin of her modest cleavage between the two triangles of her bikini top.

"Grace," he said.

"Yes, William," she replied, as though she knew what was coming. But she didn't remove her hand.

William leaned in for the kiss, but to his surprise, she lowered her face. He waited patiently. Then, after a moment, she lifted her face again. Her cheeks had grown red, but he couldn't tell whether they were reddened from the heat or from his boldness.

"This isn't the right time," she said.

"It could be."

Grace shook her head. "We're trying to achieve CA3 status as a team. Falling in love would ruin what we're trying to accomplish. You know?"

He did know. William was aware of the way that cults, for example, prohibited their members from pairing off. Some did so by allowing totally free love among everybody, others by prohibiting sex completely. Either way, the fact remained that a couple was the biggest danger to a group. And Grace was telling him that, though it would be the easiest thing in the world to form a couple with him, she didn't want to damage the team.

William scratched his face, disappointed. "What about Jeremy and Trina?"

"What about them?"

"They're almost a couple."

"No, I've talked to her. They kissed once, but both agreed that it was a bad idea. They're committed to the team, first and foremost."

William shifted on the bench, suddenly uncomfortable. She sensed his frustration and raised a hand to his face and touched his cheek gently. "You know I like you too, but the time just isn't right. We can't let ourselves fall in love."

"When will the time *be* right, Grace?" he said. "If we succeed in making it to CA3 level, then we're just going to be split up and assigned new entities. And then I'll never see you."

Grace sighed. It wasn't condescending, more out of frustration. "I don't know, William. Maybe it's our destiny not to be together." Then she grew animated, took both his hands in her own. "But don't you think we've got a higher calling? We're going to be CA3s. Not everybody can achieve that."

William hung his head. "I don't know why we can't have both."

Grace leaned over and kissed him quickly on the cheek, then stood up. "I'm going back to my room. See you in the morning."

The door opened, then closed, and she was gone. William dropped his face into his hands. He wanted the team to achieve CA3 status, of course, but he also wanted to have her, Grace, all for himself.

There *had* to be a way to make her fall in love with him.

CHAPTER 9

NEXT MORNING, SITTING IN THE GALLEY with the other members of the team, William stared down at his breakfast. It was his customary start to the day: poached egg, strip of bacon, fried potatoes, and greens. Next to him, Jeremy was eating the same, as usual, and Hunter was sucking the meat off some kind of animal bone.

Grace was on the other side of the room, chatting happily with Trina at a small side table. William had purposefully taken a seat as far from her as possible, feeling his heart torn in two. It was awful, knowing that his emotions were slaves to the whims of this girl. But his heart couldn't be pacified. He wondered if she were still thinking about their encounter last night the same way that he was.

Finally, he dared a glance at her. To his surprise, Grace was actually *eating*, not just a cup of yogurt, but a plate of food. Her face looked alive, and her skin was even glowing.

It caused a stab of panic in his heart. Was she feeling better this morning for having rejected him? Was she excited to finally be rid of him, William, this lump of sadness here on the team? Or was he overreacting?

William set his fork down and buried his face in one hand. There was a word for what he was feeling.

Love.

"So who's on deck today?" asked Jeremy.

"I am" said Trina.

"Let's make a bet about where she chooses," said Jeremy. "Tahiti? Or maybe somewhere in the Caribbean?"

"I say she picks a high tea with the queen of England," said Hunter.

"Both of you guys, shut up," she said, putting a napkin over her face. They could hear the smiling in her voice.

"Don't be upset because we know you so well," said Hunter.

She dropped the napkin, a look of astonishment on her face. "The queen of England? You know we can't snap into famous people."

"Oh yeah, says who?" said Hunter.

Hunter's tone had suddenly grown nasty, and everybody looked at him.

"Says the Ancient Engineer," replied Jeremy. "Remember the orientation? Leaders and geniuses are often too wrapped up in their own heads for us to get a sense of their lives."

Hunter dropped the animal bone on his plate. It made a hollow, clattering sound. "I'm not so sure of that."

"What makes you say that?" said Grace.

"Nothing," he said, "just a feeling. They could be lying to us."

William cleared his throat. "Come on, Hunter."

"You guys trust everything they tell us." He nearly spat the words out. "That's *pathetic*. They just make up these rules. Actually, we can do what we want."

"So you're saying that you *did* influence that Mongol yesterday?" said William.

A sneer slowly unfurled itself across Hunter's hawkish face. "What I'm saying is that we can do whatever we want on a snap."

The comment landed with a thud in the middle of the room. It lay there stinking like a dead fish.

"Hunter," said Trina, "we're in this together. Either we all advance, or none of us advances."

William wasn't sure how to insert himself into this argument. It seemed that the rest of the team was bringing up all the stresses that he'd been noticing for a very long time. It was probably better if he remained quiet.

"How do you know that's true?" said Hunter. "Think about it."

Then without waiting for a response, Hunter stood up and left the galley. The other four team members looked at one another.

"Houston, I think we have a problem," Jeremy groaned.

William made his way down to the pod tank and discovered that he had arrived first once again. As usual, the room displayed the same soft lighting, the same five pods arranged in a circle. Shana was nearby, moving some data around on the glass board.

He climbed into his customary pod. Shana heard him, took one of the cuffs, and came over to his pod.

"How was breakfast this morning?" she asked.

"Same as always," he replied, settling back, feeling the polymer beneath his head. "The only thing that really changes here is our experiences in the snaps."

"And that's by design," she replied, putting the digital cuff around his arm.

"Shana," he said, "can I ask a question?"

"You have a lot of those."

William took that as a signal to proceed. "Do we have powers in the snap that we haven't been told about?"

Her almond-shaped eyes met his. "Proof already told you in the orientation what your abilities are."

"But did he tell us *everything*?"

"Just do as we told you," she said, patting his wrist like a mother. "You'll never get to CA3 otherwise." Then she pricked his arm with the small double-tined fork.

"Ow," he said. The sensor seemed to hurt more than usual. Maybe she pushed it a little too hard.

She affixed the digital cuff to his arm, tied it, and turned it on. As the others came into the room, she went to assist them, and William lay in his pod, listening to the others entering the pod tank and thinking about her comment. He noticed that she hadn't denied his question. She'd just instructed him to do as he was told.

Then a face appeared over his pod. It was Grace.

"Hi William," she said.

He struggled to sit up. She placed her hand on his chest. "No, don't. This will only take a second. I just wanted to say thank you for being so honest with me last night."

William's jaw opened and closed as he searched for the words. He didn't know what to say, exactly. It was as though all circuit processing had stopped inside his head.

"Okay," he heard himself say.

Then she leaned into the pod and kissed him on the cheek. Her eyes were dancing as she pulled back and then disappeared. He heard her climbing into her own pod.

William clenched and unclenched his hands, feeling the heat raging across his cheek like a brush fire.

Grace liked him, but she was also playing with him.

He barely noticed when Shana slid the top shut over his face, encasing him in the pure white polymer once again. He barely saw the soft blue light run around the edges of the pod and then slowly move through the chromatic spectrum.

Finally the colored lights dimmed, and the various images of the parallax began to flicker overhead. Somewhere in the room, Trina was busy choosing one of them.

Evidently, she saw one that she liked, because the pod fell away. William was still thinking about Grace, even as he felt himself falling away, down, down, through a long tunnel, bits of light flashing past him.

CHAPTER 10

*S*NAP.

William found himself standing on a low platform before a crowd of people. His arm was in the air, finger pointed to the ceiling.

Five hundred breaths.

He was wearing a pair of brown tights with a flouncy-sleeved brocade top. A fancy hat fell down one side of his face, and his beard was trimmed to a point. Hanging from his belt was a small leather holster that held a dagger with a decorative pattern on the handle. The entire effect was foppish, that much was sure.

As he moved across the platform, he felt a small piece of metal bite into his groin. He looked down and saw a prominent bulge. That was weird.

Then he heard a strange voice speaking a language with a lot of vowels. It took a moment for him to realize it was his own voice, and that he was speaking to the crowd.

Before him, an assemblage of what appeared to be nobles and ladies were standing on the floor. Some of them were listening patiently to him, some weren't. A few of the ladies were whispering behind fans.

William realized that he was giving a speech, and it was a call for a war against the state of Venezia.

He listened to himself outlining the reasons for the aggression: the new technology, the new alliance with the papal states of Rome, and the need to bring unity to the peninsula.

Suddenly he knew when and where he was. Trina had snapped all of them into Italy, and judging from the crowd's fashion, it was the late-medieval or early Renaissance period, when the Italian peninsula was packed with warring city states. His best guess was that he was in the house of the de Medici, the famous banking family in Florence that later took political control of the city.

The crowd applauded, and he felt himself make a courtly bow. His host was flooded with relief. He turned to his left, and there sat a regal-looking man on a throne. His face was impassive, and his nose tipped slightly into the air. This was definitely somebody.

William felt himself bow again to the regent. Then he backed away.

Four hundred twelve. Four hundred eleven.

He moved through the crowd, chatting with the assembled nobles, the sophisticated people of this Italian court, feeling the other men slap him warmly on his back, and kissing the cheeks of pretty ladies.

Then he was surrounded by several exquisitely beautiful women, all courtesans. They flattered him with sweet words.

"Just a wonderful speech."

"Such passion for your city."

"Have you a wife?"

His eyes landed upon one particular courtesan, a lovely damsel with makeup on her heart-shaped face and exposed décolletage.

A nimbus encircled her head. It was orange.

Grace.

The courtesan leaned forward and kissed him on his cheek. She'd done the exact same thing back in the pod tank less than a minute ago, but when they were in different bodies. Then the courtesan pulled away and looked knowingly at him.

"What is it?" he said.

She leaned forward again and whispered into his ear. "Meet me in the refectory," she said. "Five minutes."

William nodded, then continued on. Moving through the room, William felt himself buzzing with excitement. He didn't know what or where the refectory was, but that was an invitation to a sexual rendezvous if he'd ever heard one.

He pondered his good luck for a moment. Having sex during a snap, that would be a first. It was also sex with Grace, who had tagged herself into an equally attractive woman. This was unbelievably good fortune. He wondered if there was a way that he could always snap into men who gave speeches in public. Urging war in a charismatic way was usually bad for society, but it seemed to be good way to spark a woman's interest. Although the very thought was exciting and tantalizing, something inside him resisted the idea.

William's eyes fell upon a man at the back of the crowd. He was dark, short and swarthy, with a thin moustache and piercing eyes. A black nimbus encircled his head.

Hunter.

William decided to ignore him. He didn't want to spend time considering Hunter right now. Instead, he made his way through the room, accepting congratulations and small nods of the head. This was something new for William to feel, the sensation of being the center of attention.

He arrived at a wild-eyed man standing in the corner, talking quickly and vociferously. A corona of unkempt frizzy hair was perched on his head, and his clothes were little more than rags, but his eyes were on fire with passion. Surrounding him were several people who seemed to be hanging on every word he said. One of them had a pale blue nimbus around his head.

Jeremy.

"This machine will carry humans up to the sun," the wild-eyed man was saying. "It will feature a rotor that turns like this, and it will lift us up." He lifted his hands into the air. "It will be powered with chains that the rider will move with his feet. I've made a sketch."

William heard himself say, "Those are a lot of words for someone whose engineering designs have often left the populace yearning for something a bit more substantial, Leonardo."

The man turned his gaze upon him. William immediately felt that there was something special about him, a special gift that very few had. He wondered if he was a CA3 agent.

William had thrown the gauntlet, and Leonardo accepted the challenge. "You occupy yourself with the affairs of who fights who and who makes peace with who. Those are minor details. The things that I make and design will be discussed for centuries."

"Write me a letter when it comes to pass," William heard himself say. "Our great grandchildren will thank you."

It was a snotty thing to say, and William felt himself strolling away from the group. Part of him wished that he could control his host, so that he could stay and talk with Leonardo a little more. In fact, he wondered what his host would say or do if he discovered that people in the twenty-first century would still be talking about the man he'd just mocked.

Three hundred twenty-nine. Three hundred twenty-eight.

William sauntered out of the meeting hall, down a side corridor lined with flickering torches, and entered a room with a row of seven large holes on a wooden board. Two men from the court were sitting on two of the holes with their fine hosiery rolled down to their ankles, their bare legs in the air.

William felt himself roll his own tights down to his ankles and remove the piece of metal from his crotch. He got a good look at it. This was a codpiece, not much different from goalie's cup in hockey, and it was definitely for show.

He set the codpiece on the floor and looked down into one of the holes. Cool air blew up into his face, and twenty meters below was the smooth brown surface of a river. Then William turned and sat down on the hole and felt himself begin to defecate.

Next to him, one of the other men strained hard, his face reddened with the effort.

"Drink your olive oil," offered the third man.

"It makes me sick," said the second. Then he rocked back and forth, and an expression of relief spread across his face. "At last!"

"Sweet relief," said the third. "How I wish it would visit me." William noticed that he was holding a small book in his hands.

The second man leapt to his feet. "Linen!"

A maid appeared in the room with a tray of small towels and handed him one. The second man theatrically wiped his rear end with the linen and then threw it at her. It bounced off her shirt and onto the floor.

"You are a mad animal," said the third man.

William looked at the maid. A yellow nimbus appeared around her head.

Trina.

William finished his duty and stood up and asked for a towel. Trina handed him one, which he used to wipe his backside. Then he dropped it in the canister that the woman had placed in the center of the floor.

"Civilized, that one is," said the third man.

"We must elevate ourselves above such filth as Vittorio," William heard himself say. Then he went back into the corridor without washing his hands. He supposed that was the way life was back in the day.

Two hundred forty-three. Two hundred forty-two.

He moved down the hall and arrived at the refectory. It was a long room, with a large cone-shaped hearth at the far end. The fire was roaring, and a large black cauldron hung over the orange flames. The sweet smell of meat stew filled his nostrils.

It was hot in here. William stood in the doorway and mopped the sweat from his forehead.

"Ho ladies, where has gone my Constantina?"

At a long wooden table, three female cooks were busy chopping vegetables. One looked up at him, a homely woman, and there was nearly spite in her eyes. "Why do you ask, Ludovico?"

"Because she was feeling poorly and I came to offer her my ministrations," William heard himself say.

"Certainly," said a second one, "she was feeling poorly. Of that, there is no doubt."

"Did she enter this refectory?"

"No, she did not," said one. "But she did stand right in the place where you are and announce that she was going to her quarters."

"It was a conspicuous announcement," said the third.

"Thank you, ladies," he said, grinning.

Before they could roast him any further, William left the doorway and bounded up a side stairway. A moment later, he arrived at the top floor of the castle, where it appeared the bedrooms were located. He moved down the long corridor, past the sconces, his footfalls muffled by the heavy runner carpet. He passed door after door, the iron rings built into the thick wood.

One hundred fifty. One hundred forty-nine.

William paused at one door. He knocked on it. "Constantina?" There was no response. He pushed the door open.

Inside was a suite with a four-poster bed in the corner. To his surprise, a portly man lay nude on the mattress, his fingers laced on his prodigal belly. His mouth was open and a snore emanated from his mouth.

William looked around. The room was empty otherwise. "Apologies," he said, slowly backing out of the doorway.

He shut the door and continued down the corridor.

Ninety-six. Ninety-five.

He knocked on another door. "Constantina?" he said again. No response here, either, so he pushed that door open.

He stepped inside. In this room, a man sat in the window-sill, a bottle of wine in his hand, yelling to people below. "How you wish you could be in this position, elevated above the common scrum!" he said. Then the man threw the bottle out the window. A second later, William heard it smash on the street below, and a woman cry.

Then the drunken man saw him. "Ludovico! Have you any wine from the Catalan region? I've grown so exhausted drinking this local plonk that my tongue has threatened to throw me out the window if I don't provide it with some variety."

"I have none," said William, "but I'll bring you some shortly."

"That would be most excellent!" The man clapped his hands and promptly fell off the windowsill and tumbled onto the floor.

William backed out into the corridor again. He felt himself growing impatient. It wasn't every day he was promised sex, certainly not by Grace, in whatever body, and this snap was winding down quickly.

He crept along the carpeted hallway to yet another door. He pressed his ear to the wood. A man's voice said something curt and abrupt inside. A woman gave a muffled cry.

Fifty-two. Fifty-one.

William felt himself growing curious, worried, and enraged, nearly all at once. His hands pushed the door open, and what he saw sent him reeling.

A woman lay on a divan, her face blocked by the swarthy man with the black nimbus. He was standing over her, his knee pinning down one leg, and his left hand pinning down both of her wrists over her head.

It was Hunter.

He'd almost finished ripping the clothing off the woman. Her beautiful garments were strewn on the floor, some whole, a few torn. Her breasts were exposed, and he was furiously working on the undergarments around her waist with his free hand.

"How do you open this? Tell me!" He slapped her across the face. Then Hunter's body shifted, and William got a glimpse of the woman's face.

The orange nimbus around her head was unmistakable.

It was Grace.

Twenty-four. Twenty-three.

"Ho there!" shouted William, leaping forward.

The swarthy man whirled around. His eyes went wide, and he quickly backhanded William across the face.

William fell to the floor, feeling the taste of blood in his mouth. "You haven't got the right!" he shouted.

The swarthy version of Hunter turned to Grace. "Haven't I got the right to take what I want? Haven't I?"

"No!" she cried. "You have no right to my body!"

"The world doesn't work in that way, my princess." He spat the last word out with special disdain. Then, with one yank, he tore her underpants off her body.

William gasped, averted his gaze. Grace was utterly embarrassed.

The swarthy rapist reached a hand inside his own pants and began to loosen them.

William rocketed to his feet. "Hunter, stop!" he shouted.

Time seemed to stop. Then the air in the room seemed to stretch and twist and warp, as though someone were pulling the universe like a piece of taffy. William slowly realized that he'd just committed an incredible blunder.

"Who, pray tell, is *Hunter*?" hissed the swarthy man.

"I don't know what possessed me to shout such gibberish," William heard himself say. "It was a nonsense word that came to mind."

Grace looked helplessly at William. "Ludovico, you must help me."

Seven. Six.

"Be a good lad and excuse yourself," said Hunter.

"I will not," said William, "because that woman invited me here. I'm the man with access to this bedchamber, not you."

An evil expression seeped across Hunter's face, like sewage welling up out of a drain. "If she's like most women, there's room enough for two." A vicious wink fluttered briefly at the corner of his eye.

Three. Two.

William noticed that wink. He recognized it. That was Hunter's wink, the same one he'd given William yesterday after the snap ended.

That was all the proof William needed. In that moment,

he knew that Hunter had been controlling his host. And, in this case, he'd been trying to rape Grace.

One.

The thought enraged William. He pulled the short dagger with the decorative handle from the holster on his belt and leapt forward, weapon in hand. "You bastard."

Snapback.

CHAPTER 11

WILLIAM'S EYES FLEW OPEN. THE TOP OF the pod was fixed in place directly over him, and he could feel the white goop all around him, cooling his skin. Still, he felt possessed by anger. His fingertips began to furiously claw at the translucent polymer.

"Let me out!" he shouted. "Shana!"

"Hold on!" came the muffled response.

The top slid back, and he leapt out of the pod like a deranged man.

"What are you doing?" Shana said, catching him by the arm. "I have to take off the cuff before you can go anywhere."

Steaming mad, he stopped his flight, just long enough for her to remove the digital cuff from his arm. "There," she said, "but you've still got the stuff in your hair."

William didn't listen to her. He didn't care about the goop in his hair. He had only one objective in mind. He ran to Hunter's pod and flung open the top. He looked down. It was Jeremy.

"Damn it," he said, "where is Hunter?"

Jeremy opened his eyes, startled to see him, and a little frightened at the same time. "We switched pods today."

William turned and looked across the room. At Jeremy's usual pod, Shana had slid open the top, and Hunter was starting to pull himself out.

"Hunter!" he shouted.

His teammate and supposed compatriot rolled his eyes as he unfurled his long limbs and stood himself upright on the floor.

"What is the problem now?" Hunter said in such a way that suggested William was the issue, not him.

"You know good and well what the problem is, asshole!" shouted William. He flung himself across the room and was a half-second away from Hunter when he felt Shana place herself between the two of them.

"Save it for the debriefing," she said.

William stood there, breathing. Over her shoulder, he saw Hunter affecting a casual look. He forced his breathing under control.

"Fine," said William.

The five members of the team sat sullenly in their seats, refusing to make eye contact with one another.

Proof stood before all of them, arms crossed. "Somebody had better talk, or else we're going to sit here all day." He looked at William, then to Hunter. "You two want to contribute first?"

"I don't have any problem with William," said Hunter, raising his hand, "but I think he's got a problem with me."

Proof turned to William. "Are you going to tell us the reason for this anger?"

William inhaled deeply, then slowly released the breath. "Maybe it's got something to do with the way he attempted to rape Grace in the snap."

Proof looked shocked. "Is that for real?"

"My host was trying to rape Grace's host," said Hunter.

William rocketed to his feet. "That's a load of crap! You were doing it *yourself*! You took over the host and influenced him!"

"How are you so sure that I took over that host's body?" said Hunter. "People do bad things all the time, all through history, you know? For the record, I didn't even like the feeling of it."

William felt himself trembling. "Hunter, I saw you wink at me! I recognized you in that wink!"

Hunter smirked. "Do you think people didn't wink in fifteenth-century Italy?"

William turned to Proof. "It was the *way* he winked. It was the same kind of wink that he gave me earlier, here. All I can say is that my intuition is never wrong, and my intuition told me that Hunter was controlling this man's actions." Hunter tried to interrupt, but William silenced him with a hand. "I saw him do it yesterday in the Mongolian snap, when he made that host try to steal something inside the ger."

Proof stroked his chin, as though deliberating. "Those are pretty serious charges."

Hunter stood up. "Wait, wait, I need to defend myself. There's something that William is forgetting to tell you."

Proof put out his hand and made a sit-down motion, as though willing Hunter back into his seat. "What is that?"

The others, who thus far had said nothing, turned to look at Hunter. Nobody knew whether he was going to spout a brazen lie or say something of value.

"William spoke my name," he said.

"We all say your name, quite often," said Trina.

He whirled on her. "No, he said it *in the snap*. His host was named Ludovico, and he spoke my name, right at the end. *Hunter*."

William sank his face into his right hand. That wasn't a lie. That was absolutely, completely true and he didn't realize that he'd done it until after it had slipped out of his host's mouth.

"Deny it, William," said Proof.

William lifted his face wearily from his palm. He looked around the faces, all of which were watching him. "I can't deny it," he said. "I don't know how it happened. I had no intention of controlling him or making him speak my thoughts. It just . . . came out."

Proof blew air out of his cheeks and ground the heels of his hands into his eye sockets. Then he dropped his arms by his sides. He turned around, paced the front of the room, and dragged his fingertips along the projection screen.

"You interfered in your host, William," said Proof, staring at the corner. "Humans are endowed with free will, and you interrupted that individual's free will."

"But are we?" said Jeremy. "The blank slate theory was created by people in the eighteenth-century who had almost no knowledge of physiology. We've learned since then that brain structure determines some of our behavior."

"Some," said Proof, "but not all. We still have free will. We can resist our basest inclinations. We can *change*." He looked at William. "Don't interfere with that process."

William felt himself deflate. "You're right," he said, "absolutely right. But at least I'm admitting it." One by one, he looked each of his teammates in the eye as he spoke. "I accept responsibility for what I did, even if I don't know how it happened." Then he pointed at Hunter. "But you, you're not admitting any interference. Even though I know you did it, and with bad intentions."

Hunter made a strange hissing sound. It came out of his throat, but his lips barely moved. The hair on William's neck stood up, as though a cobra had just reared up before him and announced itself.

The sound caught everyone by surprise, because it was so out of character. Proof studied Hunter for a moment, like an entomologist who'd just discovered a new species of ant. William wondered what he was looking for. Nobody knew much about Proof, except that he was an old entity, acted very smooth, and probably had a deep reservoir of knowledge about the parallax that he kept hidden. And, of course, he was their only link with the Ancient Engineer.

Hunter stopped the sound and settled back in his seat, and William relaxed once more in his seat. Satisfied that Hunter was no danger, Proof turned to Grace. "Let's hear your side of this."

"I don't know," she said, uncharacteristically miserable. "I mean, it turns out that getting sexually assaulted is no fun no matter what era you're in."

There were some low chuckles from Jeremy and Trina. Even William couldn't resist a half smile.

"Did you see any evidence of these guys interfering in their hosts?" said Proof.

"I heard William's host shout Hunter's name," she said. "That much is true. For Hunter, I don't know. It's possible that Hunter's host was trying to rape my host without any interference whatsoever. He seemed like a pretty bad guy."

William tried not to roll his eyes. While not defending Hunter, Grace was refusing to throw him under the bus. He didn't know why she wouldn't condemn his behavior. Then he realized that she hadn't seen all the circumstantial evidence that he had. She hadn't been in the ger in the previous snap, to see the odd way that Hunter's Mongol host had tried to steal the saddle. She hadn't seen his Italian host wink either, and she probably wouldn't have recognized it, even if she had seen it.

It seemed that William was out on this branch alone.

"But do you think Hunter was acting with bad intentions?" asked Proof.

"How am I supposed to know his intentions?" Grace said. "I can't know yours, or William's, or anybody's. All I can see is a person's actions."

It seemed to William that was a solid point of view. A person's beliefs or intentions were, in the end, irrelevant to the way he or she acted toward others. Our behavior was much more important. Words and thoughts just drifted up into the air like so much smoke, but actions, those crept along the earth, close to the ground, and followed a person around.

Actions speak louder than words. He grinned to himself. Those old sayings carry a lot more wisdom than people usually realize.

Then he looked over at Grace. She knew all of this. If anybody needed more evidence that she was more advanced than the rest of them, this was it.

"Hunter," said Proof, "William has just admitted his own complicity in disrupting the events of the tag-along. Would you like to make a similar admission?"

Hunter's face seemed to be drawn up into itself, like a plastic bag getting hoovered into a vacuum cleaner. "I have nothing to confess," he said.

"Nothing?"

He shook his head. It was as though Hunter were already somewhere else. His personality had vacated the room.

"You're among friends," said Proof.

"I don't see any friends here," replied Hunter.

Jeremy spoke up. "Then what do you see?"

"People who can help me get to where I'm going."

"Really?" said Grace.

"That's how you see us?" said Trina.

Hunter shrugged. "You can call it whatever you want. I want to improve my own powers."

Proof interrupted. "These are big questions, and you guys can continue this debate on your own time. Let's finish the debriefing. Jeremy, tell me what you've learned."

As Jeremy spoke, William sat back in his seat and closed his eyes. They could advance to CA3 only as a team, and right now this was looking like anything but a team.

CHAPTER 12

THAT NIGHT, WILLIAM WAS WRACKED with anxiety. He felt the tightness in his upper back, the stiffness in his neck, the anger in his throat. So he did what had worked in the past.

He went to the gym.

The Ancient Engineer had remembered to construct a small exercise room in the team quarters, down a small hallway next to the galley. It was usually empty, though Trina could be found here most regularly, cycling or running on the treadmill. Jeremy occasionally came in to use the rowing machine.

William rarely used the gym. He hadn't really needed to exercise much. Participating in a daily snap was enough activity. He didn't know exactly how it worked, but the physical activity inside another person's body seemed to have physiological results on his own. Sometimes, after a physically strenuous snap, he'd even wake up sore.

Today was different. He needed to release some of whatever had been building up in his back.

Entering the weight room, he took in the equipment. A

long rack of dumbbells of varying weights. A pull-down machine for the latissimus dorsi. A few benches, some inclined, some flat. A bench press. A pull-up bar. A squat rack.

He took a deep breath and went over to the rack of dumbbells. He selected a couple of lighter ones, twenty-five pounds, and carried them over to a bench. He seated himself on the edge, his back erect, and took one in each hand. Then, slowly, William curled them up to his chest, left, right, alternating sides. He struggled to keep his upper arms still, and held them close to his side.

On his last set, he heard a voice from the doorway. "Mind if I work out with you?"

Goosebumps went down each of Williams' legs. He knew that voice. He didn't need to turn his head, but he did anyway.

It was Hunter.

"You can do what you want, Hunter," he said, then dropped the weights on the floor. They bounced twice and rolled to a stop. "You always do."

Hunter sauntered into the room, one hand unconsciously touching his biceps, as if checking for awesomeness. William had a normal physique, but Hunter was a string bean, his limbs long, his muscles ropy and thin. Touching his own muscles was a sign of insecurity.

Hunter read the numbers on the side of the weights that William had just dropped. "Twenty-five?"

"Yes."

Hunter went to the rack and selected a pair of weights. William noticed that they were thirties. He made an annoyed face but hid it quickly. Hunter was acting like a parody of the kind of guy William didn't want on his team. Especially, when the entire team needed to progress.

He watched as Hunter sat down on the bench and lifted the dumbbells to his chest. The renegade team member admired himself in the mirror, nodding, even making kissy-face to himself. William noticed that his form was terrible.

Then Hunter dropped the weights and sat there, breathing. The silence between them was thick with tension.

Finally, Hunter turned his head. "What motivates you, William?"

That was a strange question. It wasn't challenging, or dominant, or anything. It hinted at a person who was authentically interested in others. William wasn't interested in revealing his heart to this guy. He was a scorpion after all, and you carried one of those on your back across the river at your own peril.

"Money," said William. "I want to be rich. That's why I'm here."

"I'm trying to ask you a serious question," Hunter replied.

"Maybe I don't want to answer."

"Look, I get that you don't like me," he replied, standing up. "But we're teammates. Don't you think we should at least try to get along?"

William admitted to himself that it made sense. But there was no earthly reason that he could think of to trust Hunter with his deepest thoughts and secrets.

"Honestly, I never thought too much about my motivation."

Hunter had gone over to the squat rack and was sliding

metal plates onto each end of the bar. "Most people give normal answers."

William hit upon a safe answer. "I guess that I just really want this team to succeed," he said. "And if the team succeeds, then we all advance ourselves."

Hunter positioned himself beneath the bar, his feet an appropriate distance apart, the bar pressing into his bony shoulders. "Ask yourself: What do you want to use those advanced abilities for?"

"I don't know yet," said William.

Than Hunter grunted, his legs tensing. He lifted the bar off the rack and groaned as he lowered himself to a squat, then stood up, then lowered himself, then stood up again, all with the loaded bar on his shoulders. When he reached eight repetitions, he carefully walked forward and placed the bar back on the rack.

"I would say," he replied, breathing heavily, "that it doesn't matter."

"It doesn't matter how we use our advanced abilities?" said William.

"No. What matters is that we become powerful. That's self-advancement."

William felt a chill go down his spine, as though Hunter had just casually admitted to murder. "That sounds really amoral, Hunter."

Hunter shrugged and went over to the mirror, where he flexed. "All self-advancement is good. It pushes the universe forward."

William didn't quite know what to say to that, but he

knew that it filled him with a strange fire to act. So he walked to the pull-up bar, leapt up and grabbed it, then lifted himself up so that his chin touched the bar. Then he lowered himself. He did seven more pull-ups, before falling to the floor.

He stood up, breathing hard, hands on his hips. "Or backward," he replied.

"Huh?"

"When we think only of ourselves, maybe the universe goes backward."

Hunter sneered. "Who's to say what is forward or backward? The universe is just one giant threshing machine. It chews up and spits out. It doesn't know anything else." He admired himself again in the mirror. "I'm going to be the one doing the chewing."

"Even if other people get hurt?" said William. He came over and drew close to Hunter, until they were almost nose to nose. He could smell his teammate's sweat; it carried a note of bitterness and the tangy scent of iron.

Hunter looked him up and down, and an amused smile appeared on his face. "Are we going there again?"

"You influenced your host."

He shrugged. "So did you."

"The difference is that you influenced your host to do something very bad."

Hunter's voice grew serious. He edged closer to William's face. They were nose to nose now. "Maybe I did. Maybe it's up to you to stop me, William."

"Nobody should have to suffer so that you can get your jollies."

Hunter put a hand on William's shoulder. "Life is suffering, William. Do you know who said that?"

William removed the hand from his shoulder. "Buddha. It's the First Noble Truth. Do you know the Second Noble Truth?"

Hunter kept his eyes fixed on William. "I have a feeling you're going to tell me."

"Suffering is caused by selfish craving and personal desire," said William. He poked Hunter in the sternum with an index finger. "And the third Noble Truth says that to end suffering, you must kill desire."

The importance of those words slowly sank into Hunter's brain. He looked like he was about to say something, then thought better of it. Then he turned away and strode toward the door of the gym.

Before he reached the door, however, Hunter picked up a small dumbbell from the rack and hurled it across the room.

It smashed into the mirror. William flinched, instinctively lifting his arms over his face. When he lowered them, he saw that the mirror was shattered, a spiderweb of shards of mirror, and Hunter was gone.

William stood there, scarcely daring to breath, for several more seconds. Then he shook it off and wiped his face on a towel.

Some people were simply impossible to deal with, but he couldn't write off Hunter so easily, not when William's own success depended on their cooperation.

CHAPTER 13

LATER THAT NIGHT, IN THE GALLEY, WILLIAM sat alone in the kitchen, chewing a stalk of celery, wondering why anybody would eat this useless food.

He'd been moping around for hours, obsessive thoughts floating around his brain. He worried chiefly about the interaction with Hunter earlier in the day. Going on about personal improvement no matter what the cost, no matter how many people suffer? Throwing a dumbbell at the mirror? It was egomaniacal. And it definitely wasn't the sign of someone who wanted to work for a team. William clawed his hands down the sides of his face. This conflict with Hunter was going to get worse before it got better. He knew that much for sure.

William went to the refrigerator and held open the door and looked blankly at the shelves. Nothing caught his fancy. He picked up a bunch of leafy greens, chard, maybe, or kale, then frowned and put it back. Cooking felt like too much effort, particularly when he had so much weighing on his mind. A chef who made their meals. Her name always escaped his mind, but she disappeared into her quarters after dinner and rarely spoke. If anybody on the team got the munchies at night, they had to find a way to satisfy themselves.

William shut the refrigerator door and left the kitchen and shuffled down the corridor once again, the soles of his slippered feet scraping across the floor that was as black as his mood. His shoulders slumped, and his chin was tucked into his sternum.

As William passed Grace's dormitory room, he heard a giggle, then a laugh. He paused. Something about the way that the giggle sounded made him think that she wasn't alone.

He quietly walked up to her door and gingerly laid his ear against its surface. Inside he could hear murmurings. Grace's voice.

And a low male voice.

Grace wasn't alone. He knew that voice. She was with Hunter.

William stepped back from the door, feeling the fury rising inside him. Then he fought the feeling back down. How was he supposed to spiritually advance like this? How was he supposed to feel empathy for others when he was so consumed with his own sadness, anger and anxiety? The dark sinister trio of emotions seemed to wash over him like a dark tide after every encounter with Hunter.

He stood before the door, forcing himself to breathe in, breathe out. He felt like a yogi trying to find his inner wellspring of peace. At last he felt a calm come over him. Grace was a beautiful and outstanding girl, but she was still just a girl, a human being, one with free will. She could use that free will in whatever way she liked, and with whoever she liked.

William closed his eyes. *Stay focused on the goal of advancing to CA3. The team needs unity. Focus.*

He turned away from the door, shut his eyes, and exhaled deeply. He felt a sensation of peace immediately sweep across him. It wasn't easy wrestling down the twin challenges of a disappointed teenage crush and an immense distaste for a toxic team member, but he did it.

Another sound caught his ear. It was Grace again, but this time it was like a muffled scream from inside the room. Then there was silence.

William stopped, turned around, and faced the door again.

Hunter had attacked Grace.

That was the only explanation that William could summon. The feeling of peace instantly evaporated. His field of vision narrowed; the world went red. He found himself charging toward the door, his leg flying forward, and his foot striking it.

The door burst open under the strength of his foot, and William tumbled into the room. He came to a stop and looked around. Grace was sitting on a chair at one end of the dormitory room. She was holding what looked like a small booklet in her hand.

"William!" she said. "Is something wrong?"

He turned his head. In a chair on the other side of the room sat another person, but it wasn't Hunter.

It was Jeremy, holding a similar booklet in his hand.

"I heard a scream," he said slowly, still trying to understand the situation, "and I thought there was something wrong in here. I thought maybe Hunter was here."

Jeremy and Grace exchanged looks, then both burst out

laughing. "That scream," said Grace, "was because we're *acting*." She held up the booklet. "This is a script. We're rehearsing."

William felt dazed. "Oh."

"We're acting," said Jeremy.

The red slowly drained out of William's rapidly widening field of vision. Everything was coming back into clearer focus. He hunted around for a moment until he found the right words. "Is it for a performance?"

"I guess I've made . . . a mistake," he said.

"Apparently," said Jeremy. "Hey, since you're so concerned, we're doing this because I've been having trouble feeling deeply during the snaps. Proof suggested that I practice acting."

"As a way to build empathy," added Grace.

"And she agreed to help me do a scene," Jeremy finished. "A *Streetcar Named Desire*."

William felt ridiculous. He backed slowly out of the room. "I'm very sorry to interrupt. I was just . . . worried."

"You have to fix that door," said Grace.

"I will," he promised.

"Hey, wait, before you go," said Jeremy, standing up. "Grace said you were a decent actor. Do you want to read some lines for me? Show me how to do it?"

Flattered, William stopped and thought about it. There was no harm in helping Jeremy out.

"Sure," he said.

Jeremy unfolded a third chair, and William sat down on it. Jeremy handed him the folded script. William began to read it. Then he stopped. He found himself possessed by an idea so powerful that he couldn't let go of the thought.

He handed the script back to Jeremy and stood up. "You know what, I just remembered, there's something else I have to do. Right now."

"But . . . "

William was already out the door and down the corridor. There is nothing as powerful as an idea whose time has come.

CHAPTER 14

THE NEXT MORNING, WILLIAM ARRIVED AT breakfast in the galley with an unusual bounce in his step. He was whistling a tune on his lips. Under his arm was a sheaf of neatly stapled papers.

"Well, hello," said Trina.

He nodded at her, tipping an imaginary cap. He knew full well that he was stimulating interest by appearing to carry a secret.

"What are you so happy for?" said Hunter. It came out like a snarl.

William decided to reveal that secret. "Jeremy and Grace gave me a great idea last night," he said. "Would you like to hear it?"

"Sure," said Trina.

"I have decided that in order to build our sense of empathy, we're going to put on a stage play."

"A stage play?" said Trina.

"Yes," said William.

"We don't have an audience," said Hunter.

"It doesn't matter if we don't have an audience," he replied.

"That's not the point." He nodded toward Jeremy and Grace. "They were practicing a scene last night."

Trina looked at Jeremy. "Really? You're making plays together? Weren't you going to invite anybody else?"

"It was Proof's suggestion," Jeremy said.

"He told me that it builds empathy," added Grace.

"So, after I left their room last night," said William, "I was thinking that performing a play, something where we have to be somebody different from ourselves, and listen to one another, well, it would be an excellent team-building exercise."

"It would be a good break from all these snaps," said Trina.

"Acting is harder than a snap," said Grace, "because you have to really put effort into the empathy. In a snap, you just ride the host's emotions." She looked up at William. "I think it's a great idea."

He smiled. "Thank you." Then he walked around the table, passing out the booklets to each of the team members. He'd stayed up late last night making them.

"So what play is it?" asked Trina, as she accepted the booklet. She read the title out loud. "*Oedipus Rex.* I don't know this one."

"Yeah, you do," said Jeremy. "It's the one where the guy kills his father and marries his mother, but he doesn't know it's her."

"Gross," said Trina.

"I don't want to do this," said Hunter, tossing the script on the table.

"Why not?" said Grace. "This could help us advance to CA3."

"It's, it's just . . . a stupid idea." Words evidently failed Hunter, and his face grew dark. He waved everything off.

A voice from the doorway sounded loudly, so loudly that they all jumped in their seats. "Hunter, why don't you explain your position."

William turned around. It was Proof, standing there, leaning casually against the doorframe. Everybody was a bit alarmed now; he had never come into the galley before, at least not while they were there. He was the coach and kept his distance, staying in his own quarters behind a sealed door at the far end of the hall, just beyond the pod tank.

Hunter threw down his fork. It clattered on the table. He searched for a response. "I just don't think . . . it would help . . . the *team* . . . to advance," he finally said, nearly spitting out each phrase.

"But it might help *you*," said Proof, entering the galley, circling the table. William sat down with a heavy lump in his throat. He hadn't spoken to Proof, hadn't revealed his plan. Proof must've been monitoring him, perhaps all of them. William wondered how long he'd been doing that.

"It definitely could," said Jeremy. "Just acting that one scene last night, with Grace, made me feel different."

Hunter's face contorted as he wrestled with something deep inside. Proof stood over him, like a scientist pinning down a wriggling insect. "Look, if it's the consensus of the team, I'll go along with it, okay? Whatever the team wants."

"But is it something you want?" asked Proof.

William held his breath, waiting for his response. He'd never before seen Proof so directly confront a member of the team. He wondered if their coach knew something that they didn't.

"What does that mean?" said Hunter.

Proof turned to the other members of the team. "Everybody, follow me. I want to show you something."

William and Grace exchanged looks as they stood up. This could be going anywhere. Proof seemed to read their minds. "You're not going to want to miss this."

Proof led the group down the hall to the debriefing room. Shana was already there, sitting in a chair along the wall. She had a small device in her hand. William felt the tiniest stirrings of misgivings, and for a moment, he even wondered if he could trust Proof.

"Hello, team," she said. "Please have a seat."

The five members of the team, on edge, took their customary seats. Proof walked in and surveyed the group.

"See, this is the first of your problems. You're all stuck in the same mental rut." He tapped a chair and made a swirling shape with his finger. "Everybody, get up and change seats."

"Why?" asked Trina.

"To get out of your comfort zone," he said.

None of the five moved at first. Then Proof clapped his hands. "Come on, people." They couldn't look at each other. Jeremy was the first to stand up, albeit reluctantly. Grace was next, then William, then Trina.

Hunter didn't move. His arms were crossed.

"Let's go, Hunter," said Jeremy.

"Shut up," he snarled, then slowly drew himself out of the chair.

Slowly, the five members of the team changed their seats. William chose one on the other side of the room and settled in. He understood why Proof was doing this. They'd been in this Change Agent program for a while now, and though their experiences in the snaps were fascinating, even revelatory, they'd all grown a little too comfortable here in their regular bodies and their regular patterns.

"Now," said Proof, "do you know where you all have come from?"

Nobody spoke. William had little memory of where exactly he'd been plucked from before arriving at this base. Just a vague impression of a large box, though he might've imagined that, too. Sometimes he thought he had memories from his life, but they turned out to be stories other people told him. He wondered if he was the only person who experienced this.

"It's a place called Menoram," said Proof. "Do you remember what your life was like there?"

Nobody spoke. William had been told that Menoram was a warehouse of sorts, a spiritual waiting room, but he drew a blank when he thought of it.

"I don't think we remember anything," said Grace.

"You don't," said Proof, "because you did not accumulate any memories prior to coming to the parallax. Did you know that?"

The group slowly shook their heads.

"Now, I'm going to show you something that you will

never forget, just so you can see what's at stake for you on this team."

He nodded to Shana. She pressed a button on the device. The entire wall of the debriefing room lit up. It was a seemingly endless collection of compartments, a dihedral superplex. The sky was a bright unearthly orange, and little slivers of light pulsed between each of the compartments.

"That's Menoram," said Proof, "and those are the spirit chambers. Each one contains a different spirit. Raise the perspective, Shana."

Shana touched the device, and the point of view on the wall began to lift up and pull back. William could see that this field was not small. Menoram was in fact a vast field of spirit chambers, containing thousands, millions, perhaps even billions.

William watched the scene, stupefied.

"You have been selected from that group," said Proof. "Out of billions of spirits, yours have been identified as the most likely to progress. In fact, it's from spirits such as yours that the human race will improve itself."

The others had fallen silent. Finally Jeremy said, "Are we supposed to say thank you?"

That broke the heaviness of the moment. He could always be counted on for a good punchline at a crucial moment. Trina laughed out loud, Grace smiled silently, and William stretched his arms over his head and exhaled. Hunter just sat there, sullen, arms crossed, silent.

"Thank the Ancient Engineer!" said Proof.

Hunter lifted a questioning finger. "So why are you showing us all of this?"

Proof answered immediately. "For one reason: if this team doesn't progress to CA3, all of you will return to Menoram. And you won't have this opportunity again. You'll be back in the cycle of ordinary spirits, for the rest of eternity." He looked at the members of the team. "So here's what I want. Right now, I want your *verbal commitment* that you are going to help every member of this team succeed. I'll start with Grace." He turned to her. "Do you promise to help this team succeed?"

She nodded. "I promise."

Proof turned to Jeremy. "Jeremy?"

"I promise."

"Trina?"

"Yes."

"William?"

"Absolutely."

Then Proof turned toward the fifth member of the team. He'd intentionally saved Hunter for last. "And you?"

Hunter smiled, revealing two rows of sharp white teeth. It was a guilty smile, a false smile, a smile that told everybody the words coming out of his mouth would be pretty little lies.

"I want everyone on this team to succeed," he said.

"Good," said Proof. He produced the copy of the play from his desk and handed it back to Hunter. "To make that happen, we all have to *work* as a team. Okay?"

"You bet," said Hunter, giving Proof a thumbs-up.

Proof looked at him for a minute, trying to gauge if he was serious or mocking. His tone was impossible to tell. Then he turned to the group. "You're free to return to the galley and finish your breakfast. Shana will see you in the pod tank in twenty minutes."

Then he left the debriefing room. The others, who had barely dared to breathe during the confrontation, now exhaled.

"Wow," said Jeremy. "We just saw heaven. That was the afterlife."

Trina turned to Shana. "Can you show us that again?"

Shana nodded. "Sure, but it never changes." The image appeared on screen once again, and the team stared at the vast field of spirit chambers. Then Shana added, "Also, you have one thing wrong. You're not looking at the afterlife. It's the *before* life."

A movement caught William's eye, and he turned his head.

Hunter's seat was empty. He'd left the room.

CHAPTER 15

FOUR HOURS LATER, DURING THE PLAY rehearsal, William clutched the hair on the sides of his head, wondering why he'd ever had this stupid idea.

The play rehearsal hadn't gone as smoothly as planned. True, the team had gathered in the common area. True, the team members were sitting in a tight circle, holding the printed sides. True, they'd at least made it partway through a rehearsal for a play that would be performed for nobody, but themselves. But they'd been arguing a bit more than usual.

"Start from the top," said Jeremy. "Trina, you begin."

She spoke in an exaggerated dramatic voice. *"My king, I swear I'm not the murderer. I cannot point him out. As for the search, Apollo forced us to do it. He should name the killer!"*

Hunter stifled a laugh. Trina stopped and glared at him. "What is so funny?"

"You're a really bad actress," he said.

"Let's hear you read the line, smart-ass."

Hunter smirked. "No."

William stepped in. "Hunter, this isn't about the quality of the acting. It's about getting into the spirit of the character." He wanted to say a lot more but held his tongue. "Okay, let's skip ahead to where Tiresias is confronting Oedipus."

"What are they fighting about?" asked Jeremy.

Grace said, "Tiresias is an old blind prophet. Oedipus asks him to identify who killed Laius, but Tiresias says he won't do it. So Oedipus gets furious and accuses him of doing the murder."

"What a loser," said Trina.

"I'll play Tiresias," said William, "and Hunter, you play Oedipus."

Hunter sighed in exaggerated frustration. "I want Grace to start."

"Fine," said William. "But Hunter, you take over at line three seventy-six."

Grace cleared her throat and began to read in a clear, noble voice. "*The crown the city gave me—I never wanted it. They put it in my hands . . .*"

William listened to her as she continued. Grace was a natural-born actor, not in mimicry, but in finding the emotional center of a character. And none of them had had much time to read the sides, mark them up, or practice. This was her first time through the scene, and she'd understood the character quickly, without much effort. It was a gift.

He listened as she finished the monologue. "*Rescue yourself. Rescue your city. Rescue me. Rescue everything touched by the dead. We're in your hands, Tiresias. Helping others with all his gifts and strength is the most noble thing a man can do.*"

When she finished, Trina and Grace broke out into small excited applause.

"That's great," said William, "and now let's have Hunter pick up with the Oedipus part."

"What line again?"

"Three seventy-six. This is where Oedipus starts to get angry at the blind man because he's not cooperating."

Hunter drew himself up in his chair. William watched him try to inhabit another person. He read in an artificially loud and angry voice. "*Tiresias! You know the identity of the murderer and you won't tell me? Do you want to destroy Thebes? Do you want to destroy me?*"

William noted that the last sentence wasn't in the script. Hunter had improvised that personal injury. William answered with the blind prophet's line. "*I don't want to cause pain for either of us. So why this interrogation? You can't get anything from me.*"

Hunter grew enraged. "*I can't get anything from you! You're scum! You would make a stone furious! You don't want to talk? Spit it out!*"

As Tiresias, William remained calm. "*Don't criticize my temper, because the one you have to live with is apparently even worse.*"

Hunter was now authentically angry. The other team members were shrinking back from him. William understood what was happening: Hunter couldn't emotionally differentiate between the character's words and his own self.

"*Who wouldn't lose his temper talking to you? You want this city to burn!*"

William crossed his legs in his chair, like a Zen master. "*What will come, will come.*"

"*If you know what will come, you must tell me. Don't deny me!*"

His anger was palpable. William admitted to himself that pretending to be an egotist who wouldn't be satisfied came naturally to Hunter.

"*I won't say any more. Do whatever you want, build your anger, raise your rage.*"

Hunter shot to his feet and flipped over his chair. Trina screamed, then clapped a hand over her mouth. He continued: "*Oh, I'll let it all out. I have such incredible fury. I can see it all. You hatched the plot. You did this. You arranged the murder—and I'd bet that if you had eyes, you'd even killed him yourself!*"

"*No,*" said William, "*I say that you are the murderer. The one you are pretending to look for.*"

Hunter looked at him with enraged eyes. William sensed that they'd crossed some kind of line, the one that had been drawn between reality and make-believe.

They held the silence for a few awkward seconds. Grace was the first to break in. "Maybe that's enough for right now?"

Hunter threw his paper into the middle of the group and stormed out of the living area. He stopped at the door and turned around and hurled an accusatory finger at William. "I didn't kill him. *You* did, William. *You* did."

William froze. Trina's eyes grew wide, and Grace's face turned white. William realized that Hunter had gone off the deep end.

Finally Jeremy cleared his throat and played peacemaker. "It's just a play, bro. Why don't you go settle down?"

"I'll do whatever the hell I want!" Hunter screamed. He threw the palm of his hand against the door, rattling it in its frame. He disappeared, and the other four team members listened to his ranting grow fainter as he moved down the corridor.

Grace turned to William. "Maybe we shouldn't perform this play after all."

William's hands found their way back to the hair at the side of his head. "Yeah, that's probably for the best."

CHAPTER 16

LATE THAT NIGHT, WILLIAM LAY IN HIS bed, a heavy book on his lap. He'd always been a big reader, particularly novels in the genres of science fiction, fantasy, and even horror. Since joining this team, however, he found himself reading even deeper stuff, particularly philosophy and historical fiction and nonfiction. The small library in the galley provided some challenges in those areas. So far, he'd plowed through *Being and Time* by Martin Heidegger, made it through half of *War and Peace* by Tolstoy, and skipped Kant's *Critique of Pure Reason*.

At the moment he was paging through Gibbon's *History of the Decline and Fall of the Roman Empire*, deciding if it was worth a deeper read, when a pair of voices in the hallway caught his ear. It was pretty late for anyone to be awake, let alone having a conversation.

He went over to his door and opened it, just a crack. Then he bent down and listened. He heard feet shuffling quietly along the floor and two male voices talking quietly. It was Proof and Hunter.

William listened as the voices receded. Burning with curiosity, he crept out of his room, being careful to close the door quietly, and moved down the corridor. The voices were coming from the debriefing room.

He padded up to the door, which had been left slightly ajar, and peeked in. Proof and Hunter were sitting in a pair of chairs, turned slightly apart at forty-five-degree angles, and having what seemed to be an intense conversation.

"What this team understands," said Proof, "is that there's more to life than what you can see right in front of you."

Hunter was shaking his head. "We're all different."

"Not in some ways, man. This team shares common goals, common ways of behavior, common boundaries."

"You're just talking and talking, but the words just don't make sense."

Proof reached forward and tried to touch Hunter's shoulder. "Do you understand that people have boundaries? It's true. These things called boundaries exist, and they exist for a *reason*."

Hunter was staying surprisingly calm. "What they and you consider normal behavior is not what most people consider normal."

Proof removed his hand from Hunter's shoulder and sat back, frustrated. In the corridor, William crouched down and hugged his arms around his knees. Nobody had said anything about a late-night counseling session, not Proof, not Shana, not anybody on the team. It must've been kept secret on purpose. He wondered how many one-on-ones there had already been between these two. It also reassured him to know that

Proof possibly viewed Hunter as the weak link in the chain.

Proof rubbed his forehead. "Listen, there was a philosopher in the mid-eighteenth century named Ralph Waldo Emerson. Have you heard of him?"

Insolent, Hunter just made a blah-blah-blah motion with his hand. Undaunted, Proof went on. "I'll take that as a no."

"Emerson believed in pure individualism," said Proof, "but with the addendum that each individual was part of the greater oversoul." He paused. "He wanted the best of both philosophies. He wasn't too far off the truth, you know."

Hunter spun around in his chair, clearly losing patience. "So, why are you bringing all this to me?"

"Because you ought to read him, understand him. *To appreciate beauty, to find the best in others, to leave the world a little bit better, to know that even one life has breathed easier because you have lived.* That, he said is success."

"Didn't he talk about goblins too?" Hunter said.

It took Proof a moment to remember. "Yes, he did. Hobgoblins. Something about fools and consistency."

Hunter huffed. "Weirdo."

They both fell silent. William remained crouched in the hallway, scarcely daring to breathe. He imagined that doing counseling sessions with Hunter must be one of the most useless activities in the world.

"I could just send you back to Menoram," said Proof. "It is a possibility."

"And condemn me to an eternity of normalcy? What a punishment."

"Look," said Proof, leaning forward in his chair, running

his hand through his hair, "you know you're a difficult guy, right?"

"Whatever you say, boss."

"Here's something that you may not have thought of. There are other powerful forces that exist."

Hunter paused, and William could see through the cracked door that his teammate had grown concerned.

"What does that mean?" Hunter said.

"It means that if you continue acting out, you might attract the attention of some fallen entities. And we won't necessarily choose to help you if anything goes wrong."

Hunter sat up in his seat, and a note of panic or desperation seeped into his voice. "Is that a threat?"

"Not at all."

"But I thought you and the Ancient Engineer were, like, omnipotent."

Proof rubbed his forehead. "Maybe so, but there are other entities that once worked side-by-side with us. They also are very powerful, especially in the area of deception. The Ancient Engineer is all powerful, true, but there are things you just don't understand. Since you are operating in a free-will environment, these other entities can still come and go. So if something decides to come here," he said, making a circle in the air with his finger to indicate the team's quarters, "and interfere with us, your actions leave you very vulnerable."

Hunter thought about that, his mouth working in little movements, his eyes going leftward and upward. Then he seemed to make up his mind. "I can handle them."

"Why do you say that?"

"Because I'm becoming a CA3." He lowered his voice, conspiratorially. "I have powers."

Proof leaned forward and lowered his voice. "You have nothing that hasn't been given to you. But remember this, your teammates have also received powers."

"But my powers are greater," he boasted.

Proof waved a dismissive hand, then got to his feet. "You're not hearing anything that I'm telling you."

"Aww, come on. I thought we were going to be friends," mocked Hunter.

"Good night," said Proof.

He moved toward the door. In the corridor, William scrambled to his feet and ran silently down the hallway. As he turned the doorknob to his room, he heard his name.

"William." He turned. It was Proof.

"Yes."

"You were listening to us?"

William chewed his lip, his hand still on the door. He decided not to risk a lie. "Yes, I was."

Proof nodded. He regarded William for a moment, as though from a great distance. "You can go to bed now."

"Yes, Proof."

William entered his room and shut the door behind him. He stood with his back against the door, breathing heavily.

CHAPTER 17

SNAP.

Next morning, William found himself running across a prairie. The sun was low on the horizon, probably sunset, if he had to guess. He was naked except for a leather loincloth. His skin was black, and in his hand was a spear. He could feel something in his lip.

Five hundred breaths.

The thick tufts of weeds felt tough beneath his feet, but he barely noticed. The calluses must be thick. He felt himself running lightly, so lightly that it was as though he were drifting across the ground, rather than touching it.

To his right, a black man was running, slightly hunched over. He wore nothing except a loincloth that covered his genitals but left his buttocks bare. In the distance, a purple mountain was capped by a small ring of white clouds. The ground was littered here and there with the bleached-white bones of an animal.

This was definitely Africa. Not the Africa of safaris and Range Rovers and glamorous tents and fruit smoothies at dusk, but the original continent itself, untouched by human development. William wondered what year they'd landed in. It didn't really matter. This was primitive.

A yelp sounded from the left. William turned his head. Another man, crouched on a nearby ridge, was cupping his mouth with one hand and pointing with the other. Evidently he was acting as a spotter, because William and the other man both adjusted their course, toward the indicated direction.

They arrived at a fallen tree that, with its twisted, gnarled roots poised high in the air, looked like a surrealist painting. From the other side of the tree came the horrific squealing sound of an animal.

They skirted the edge of the roots and stopped. Several other members of what William assumed was his tribe had cornered a giant peccary, or warthog, in the space where the tree and the side of the ridge met. The animal had sharp tusks, sported a coat of glossy but bristly hair, and stood nearly waist high on a man. It was bellowing ferociously.

Five men stood around it, their spears drawn. William ran to join their ranks, as did the other man. Now it was seven spears.

Someone shouted a command.

The other men shouted a response.

A single shout, in unison.

William felt himself hold his breath, dart forward, plunge his spear into the animal's neck, and then dart back to the line. The peccary's squealing grew twice as loud, and the fur around the animal's neck was now drenched in blood. It spun in a crazed circle, spraying its blood in every direction.

Four hundred twenty-two. Four hundred twenty-one.

Another tribe member ran forward and plunged his spear into the animal's hindquarters. It squealed again and spun around and caught the man's heel in its jaw. The man fell to the ground, his white eyes wide with fright.

"No!" William heard himself shout, and a feeling of panic and concern raced through his body.

Then the nimbi appeared. He was wondering why he hadn't seen them yet. The men with him displayed yellow, pale blue, and black nimbi: Trina, Jeremy and Hunter.

The man on the ground had an orange nimbus.

It was Grace.

William cried out. Without thinking, he rushed forward and leapt onto the animal's back. It smelled awful, the rude stench of pure animal mixed with the sharp, tangy scent of fresh blood.

The peccary let go of Grace's leg, and her host scrambled away, the man's blood mixing with the animal's blood on the ground. The peccary spun around, frantically trying to turn its head to reach William, but he'd wrapped his arms around the animal's neck. This was a ridiculous situation. He couldn't let go, but he couldn't hang on either

"William! Get off him!" a voice in his head shouted.

He froze. Who had just spoken?

"Who is that?"

"It's me, Grace! Get off that animal so we can kill it! They're afraid of spearing you!"

He was confused. *"How are you speaking to me?"*

"I don't know!"

Another voice butted in. *"Guys, we're all hooked up now!"* It was Jeremy.

"What about Trina?"

"Here" came her response.

"Hunter?" said William.

"I wish you could see how insane you look," said Hunter's voice.

William looked at all the faces. They were having a telepathic conversation while occupying the bodies of other people.

"She's right," said Jeremy. *"My host won't move until he knows he won't kill you."*

William couldn't influence his own host. He hoped that the man would be smart enough to fling himself off the back of the peccary.

In the end, it didn't matter. The warthog began to stagger from the loss of blood and the weight of William's host's body. A moment later, it collapsed, falling on its side and pinning William beneath all four hundred pounds of its weight. He felt the breath being squeezed out of him.

Two hundred forty-nine. Two hundred forty-eight.

He felt hands under his armpits, pulling him out from beneath the mortally wounded animal. He felt himself pulled across the dirt to the shade of the tree. He felt the hot, sticky blood smeared all over his chest and arms. He felt his hyperventilating lungs finally slowing down, returning to normal.

He looked up and saw several members of the tribe standing over him, including the ones with the orange and yellow nimbi.

"You look unbelievable," said Trina. *"I'm taking a picture in my mind."*

A telepathic shout from nearby: *"Chow time!"*

That voice belonged to Hunter. They all looked over. Hunter was hacking the leg off the motionless peccary with a giant axe. It was savage.

"Wow," said William.

The others helped William to his feet, and then he watched as they joined Hunter and cut the animal into several large pieces. They tied the chunks of meat to three long poles. In pairs, the group hoisted the poles onto their shoulders and carried the meat across the savannah.

One hundred ten. One hundred nine.

William followed the line of tribesmen, still covered in the dried warthog blood, feeling very much like a butcher. Exhausted, happy, at one with the universe.

Up ahead, the tribesman with the black nimbus reached forward and tore off a piece of raw meat from the animal's haunch and stuffed it into his mouth.

"Give us a report," said Jeremy.

"It's perfect," said Hunter. *"This is the way I always want to eat."*

William ran a finger across the blood on his chest and put the finger in his mouth. The taste of hot animal blood zinged through his mouth and wakened something ancient in him.

"Man, that's good," he said.

"Isn't this disrespectful," asked Grace, *"the way we're just talking over these people's experience?"*

"Who cares?" said Trina. *"We've progressed, or something."*

They continued across the savannah, the shadows of the bushes lengthening on the ground as the orange disk sunk ever closer to the western horizon. Nearby, an animal howled. Overhead, a dozen carrion birds circled, tracking the humans' progress.

Fifty-seven. Fifty-six.

One of the birds suddenly swooped down and attacked one of the tribesman. It was Hunter. The bird pecked at his face and eyes. Hunter dropped his end of the pole, shielding his face with his hands, and the fresh meat fell onto the dirt.

"Aaahhhh!" he shouted.

The four tribesmen who weren't carrying the poles ran to Hunter's host, as the other carrion birds dove down and surrounded the meat on the ground, tearing at it with their beaks.

The tribesmen stabbed at the birds with their spears, whooping and crying. But the birds were so large that they weren't deterred. Several, in fact, fought back, attacking with beaks and claws. One slashed Trina across the leg, and she screamed in pain.

Twenty-four. Twenty-three.

"William, get over here!" shouted Jeremy.

William replied, *"I can't influence my host!"*

Hunter's host was on the ground now, being attacked by the bird. It was standing on his chest, eating one of Hunter's eyeballs.

"What the hell," said Hunter, *"somebody help me!"*

Finally, William could take no more. He forced his host to lift his spear and run toward the gruesome scene.

Nine. Eight.

William heard himself shout something, and then with a tremendous force of will, he launched the spear at the bird.

It missed, went wide, clattered in the dirt. The bird looked up, an eyeball hanging by a cord from its miserable little face. The bird spread its wings and launched at William.

"No!" shouted William.

Three. Two.

He lifted his hands to protect his face.

One.

The animal's beak tore into the flesh of his hands.

Snapback.

CHAPTER 18

AN HOUR LATER, THE ENTIRE TEAM WAS sitting in the debriefing room, all five talking at once. Proof stood before them, playing traffic cop, trying to get an accurate explanation of what had happened.

"So let me get this straight," he said. "This bird attacked Hunter's host, and pulled his eyeball out."

"It hurt like hell," said Hunter. "What a ferocious animal."

"And then William's host went forward to rescue, and then the bird turned and attacked William's host."

Trina raised her hand. "My guy felt confused about why William's host would do that."

"Mine too," said Grace. "My host thought something like, why do you help him, the man is already going to die?"

"It was that bird," said Jeremy. "My host was thinking how nobody ever challenges that bird. I don't think helping a fallen tribesman was something that they were accustomed to seeing."

Proof swiveled back toward Hunter. "You look like you've got something important to say."

"This tribe," said Hunter, nearly spitting out the last word, "is happy to watch another man get eaten by a giant bird of prey."

"Yes," Proof said.

"No wonder they're primitives," Hunter said.

William saw Proof briefly clench his hand into a fist, then relax it again. Still, his face and demeanor remained calm. "Careful not to judge them, Hunter. Ask yourself: what can you *learn* from this tag-along?"

Hunter's face hardened into an angry, mangled expression. "Not to trust any of you."

There was a stunned silence in the room. "Oh, come on," said Jeremy.

Hunter turned in his seat and swept a long, accusatory finger across the room. "I think you all did this on purpose."

"Are you serious?" said William. "It was just bad luck that you snapped into somebody who got eaten by a bird."

Trina giggled, then clapped a hand over her mouth.

A strange, wicked fire lit up Hunter's eyes as they darted around, glaring at each of the five other faces in the room. "No, I think somebody here is trying to hurt me. Someone in this room."

"Hunter," said William, "with all due respect, you're being totally ridiculous."

"Am I?"

"Yes, nobody was out to get you. In fact, I risked my life and tried to *save* you." Too late, William realized that he'd basically admitted to having influenced his host. He decided to change the subject.

He sat up in his seat and straightened an imaginary pile of

index cards in his palms. "Proof, there's something else we haven't told you yet. We all discovered a new power on this snap."

"Do tell," said Proof.

The team members looked at one another. "Who wants to say it?" said William.

"We can communicate telepathically," said Grace.

They watched Proof for his reaction. Sure enough, he appeared taken aback. "Already?"

Jeremy nodded. "We were talking to one another through the whole thing. Comments, jokes, everything."

Proof looked to the others, who all nodded. "Do you still have that power here?"

"I don't know," said Jeremy, "but we could test it out." He swiveled toward William. "Think of a color, and we'll all say it."

William closed his eyes. *Fuchsia*. Then he opened his eyes. "Everybody got it?"

They nodded.

"Okay, on the count of three. One, two, and . . . "

"Fuchsia," said the other four simultaneously.

Proof sat down in his chair. "Well, this changes everything."

"Are we in trouble?" said Grace.

"No, not at all," replied Proof. He stroked his chin. "I'm going to have to talk to the Ancient Engineer." Then he clapped his hands on his thighs. "Okay everybody, that's all for today."

"Aren't you going to use the spectrometer?" asked Grace.

"No, that's for beginners," he said, "and I think you're all past that stage. But as usual, what do we know about the Ancient Engineer?"

In unison, the group said, "He loves us, and he wants us to succeed."

Proof snapped his fingers, and the lights dimmed. "We'll reconvene later."

The team stood up. William caught Hunter by the shoulder and whirled him around. "That's the last time I try to help you," he said.

Hunter sneered and turned away.

CHAPTER 19

THAT NIGHT, AS SHANA'S VOICE CAME over the overhead intercom, William set down his copy of the *Bhagavad-Gita* on his chest.

This was alarming.

She'd used the system only once before, when there was an infrastructure malfunction in the galley and she needed to warn everyone to stay away. In truth, there really wasn't much need for an intercom, since, with only five team members, she could easily knock on the doors of their rooms. So Shana's taking to the intercom was something special indeed.

Her voice began: "Team members, please note that we're hosting a special meeting in the debriefing room in thirty minutes. Your presence is mandatory. Again, special meeting in the debriefing room in thirty minutes."

The intercom clicked off. William lay on his bed, the reading lamp perched over his shoulder, for a minute longer. Then he rolled off walked across the room toward his bathroom. It was plain, but well equipped. William looked at his face in the mirror. He inspected the skin beneath his eyes, then turned his face from side to side.

What did his team think of him? What kind of person did they think he was?

He always tried to do unto others, as the saying went. He understood that his role in the universe was to help other people improve theirs. To scratch one another's back. But maybe he'd gotten the order wrong. Was it possible there were people who viewed life in a totally different manner? Who viewed other humans as obstacles to happiness? Or, even worse, as threats to be extinguished?

William washed his face and brushed his teeth and combed his hair. Then he picked out a new shirt. They'd all been issued standard clothing upon arrival, five shirts and five pants, but William kept one pair in reserve. He believed that special moments deserved special outfits.

He reached into his bureau and pulled out that one outfit, a navy blue T-shirt with gray dungarees.

A half hour later he arrived at the debriefing room. The others were already there, waiting, a harsh atmosphere in the room.

"You guys look like you're going to your own executions," he said.

"This can't be good, bro," said Jeremy, biting a fingernail. "I mean, she used the *intercom.*"

Trina giggled a little, but Grace turned on her. "Take this seriously. We're all worried."

William thought that Grace was overreacting to the issue. He turned to Hunter. "Hunter, are you worried about this meeting?"

"Nope," said Hunter. "I just keep telling myself that the

Ancient Engineer loves us and wants us to succeed." There was a hint of mockery in his voice.

Jeremy re-entered the conversation. "Guys, the worst thing that happens is that we go back to Menoram and forget that any of this ever happened. Maybe that's what the announcement is about."

"And another hundred cycles of lives before we get selected again," added Trina.

Footsteps sounded behind them. They turned their heads to see Proof enter the room. He wore a determined look on his face, and William thought he detected a bit of a smile.

"It looks like they're all here," he said. "How wonderful."

"As requested, sir," said Hunter, snapping into a salute. He did it with such malice that everybody was taken aback.

Proof studied him, but didn't take the bait. "Thank you, Hunter." The coach went to the front of the room, settled into his seat, then rubbed the bridge of his nose. It was a gesture of exhaustion.

"What's this about, Proof?" asked Grace.

"As you know." Proof began.

That put William's antenna up. Nobody begins a nice meeting by saying, "As you know." That is usually what people say just before they fire an employee.

"You have been scheduled, and pursued, a long list of daily tag-alongs in the pursuit of CA3 designation. Right? That has been the agreement?"

The five team members nodded.

"Well, there's been a slight modification to the plans," he said, "by the order of the Ancient Engineer."

A hush settled over the room while the team waited for the other shoe to drop. Proof's eyes scanned all of them as though he were trying to peer into their souls.

Finally, Trina broke the silence. "Well? What is it?"

Proof held up three fingers. "You have only three more tag-alongs to advance to CA3 status."

The silence returned, blanketing the room. Jeremy covered his eyes. Hunter stretched out his arms and legs like a cat awakening from a nap. Trina looked like all the blood had drained out of her face. Grace didn't move.

William, meanwhile, grew curious about the mechanism for the advancement. He raised his hand. "Proof, you guys haven't been exactly clear with us about the advancement. How do we know when we've reached it?"

"The algorithms," came the coach's reply. "The Ancient Engineer has meticulously laid out the process of spiritual advancement in a system. It works."

"But how?" asked Jeremy. "We don't know the system, or the algorithms. How do we know when we've qualified?"

The others agreed, their voices rising. Proof hushed them. "The best I can tell you is that you will know it when it happens."

"Can you give us a *clue*?" said Trina.

"We're just flying blind otherwise," added Jeremy. "Also, some of us are more advanced than others." He looked around. "Come on, guys, we're all thinking it."

Next to him, Trina nodded. The two of them, she and Jeremy, had been dragging for quite a while, the caboose of the team, and everybody knew it.

Proof thought about the request. "Okay, here's my advice, make your own decisions. Be yourselves."

"That's it?" asked William.

"It's exactly that simple," said Proof, "and exactly that hard. Let me explain with a metaphor. You know how sometimes you hear a musician who makes totally amazing songs? That person's art is unique, and nobody else in the world does it like that?"

All five members of the team nodded.

"That person is self-actualized. It's the only way to succeed. Just be yourselves, and make decisions that are true to your higher calling."

"While we're being other people," said Hunter, smirking.

It was a good point, and Proof turned to him, finger on chin. "Ironically, Hunter, we learn to be ourselves by immersing in other people's experiences for a short period of time. That's what stories are all about, really. Learning about other people's decisions to help your own."

Proof turned back to the others. "So, on tomorrow's snap, I want you to focus on doing what I just described. Really try to feel how your host makes decisions. Keep the chatter to a minimum. You know what I mean."

Everyone grinned. They knew they'd talked a lot in the last snap, maybe too much.

"As usual, what do we know about the Ancient Engineer?" said Proof.

"He loves us, and he wants us to succeed," the group said wearily. As William left the room, he wasn't so sure that was true.

After all, three snaps didn't feel like much time. And now the pressure was on.

CHAPTER 20

"WILLIAM," SAID SHANA'S VOICE.

He jerked up in his seat. William had set-tled himself in the team's small auditorium and was staring at the moving pictures on the wall. It was not unlike a cinema, except the flickering images on the walls were part of the parallax. Specifically, these were dreams that peo-ple were having, in different eras, in different cultures all over the world. Watching them was like working for extra credit. William and the others were encouraged to spend time here, in the continuing effort to see the world from others' points of view.

"What?" he said. He turned around and saw Shana in the doorway. "Oh, hey."

"Are you busy?" she asked.

He gestured at the parallax. "Define busy."

"Proof wants to talk to you."

He put an index finger on his sternum. "Me? Now?"

Shana smiled. "In his private office. Come on." She held the door of the room open, waiting for him.

William felt a cold sweat break out across his body. He

knew he broke a rule by influencing his host in the last snap, and that he had admitted to it. He could only imagine what type of punishment Proof might be cooking up for him. Maybe he'd be sent back to the big Jacuzzi of souls to spend another quality millennium in his spirit chamber. Maybe he'd been relegated, dropped down a level, down to CA1. Or maybe he'd be denied entry to CA3, along with the entire team. He shuddered at the thought.

"All right," he said.

William followed Shana out of the auditorium and through the corridors. They arrived at Proof's gate. It was marine blue, and a small ball of light pulsed in a slow circumference around the aperture, like a guard marching the perimeter. Nobody on the team had been allowed through it. Ever since they arrived here, William and the rest of the team had been wondering aloud about what lay beyond the gate.

Nearby was a small desk, like a receptionist's. Shana seated herself on the chair at the desk, typed a couple of words onto a screen, and then reached over and waved her hand in front of the aperture. It dissolved, and the entire door jamb was framed by a thin line of light. Shana gestured for him to step through.

"Is it safe?" asked William.

"It's weird to see you asking a dumb question," she said. "You're not in trouble. Proof asked you to come. So go on, get inside!"

Taking a deep breath, William passed through the aperture. It closed behind him. He took another step forward and felt everything fall away. He whirled around. Shana wasn't there. The desk wasn't there. Even the doorway was gone. William looked down at his arms. They weren't there either. There was nothing here except the emptiness of space and time.

"*William,*" said a voice.

It was a familiar voice being communicated telepathically.

"*Proof?*" William replied. He didn't know how he was forming words, since he no longer had a mouth, tongue or throat.

"*Don't move.*"

William froze. A small green light moved toward him across the nothingness. It arrived in the shape of Proof.

"*Are you alone?*"

"*Who else would I have brought?*"

A spotlight beamed out of Proof's eyes and roved across his body. "*You're not shaking yet. That means you're handling it okay. But if you start to vibrate, I have to send you back.*"

"*Okay,*" said William.

Proof swept a hand around the vast void. "*Welcome to my humble abode. A pleasure to show somebody what I see.*"

"*I thought you were mad at me.*"

"*For what?*"

"*Spying on you. Interfering with a host during a snap. I haven't been the best team member.*"

He heard Proof emit what sounded like a sigh. "*Interfering with a host is natural, William. During my experiences, I did it too. Mostly it's a sign that you're getting ready to advance.*"

"*I can feel it,*" said William.

"*It's very clear to the Ancient Engineer.*"

That surprised him. *"He's been watching us?"*

"Sometimes. We talk about who is making the most progress, who has outstanding potential. I told him that you're one of them. So is Grace."

William felt reassured. Around him rotated a constellation of stars. *"So, why did you want to talk to me?"*

Proof didn't answer right away, so William waited. He could hear a low throbbing, almost out of the range of hearing. It sounded like a distant electronica concert.

Proof finally replied. *"Do you have experience with evil?"*

"No, I can't say so."

"Look at this and tell me what you see."

A long parallax, much like a mural, began to pass before William. It showed humans in various stages of aggression and anger. A contorted face, mouth open in a baboon-like pucker. A fist crushing into a chest. A man squeezing the trigger on a pistol. Explosions. Angry shouts.

"Tell me what you see."

William struggled to find something incisive to say. *"I don't know. These people seem to be angry, but they don't seem evil."*

The image disappeared, and Proof appeared once more. *"That's very astute, William. Angry people aren't evil. They've just been hurt or damaged."*

"So then why did you ask me about evil?" said William.

"Watch."

Another long parallax appeared before William. He saw people walking, talking, laughing. Playing with children in parks. Laboring in fields. Typing at computers.

Proof explained: *"Those people have all submitted them-*

selves, and their souls, to something larger than themselves. They are pursuing transformation from self to selflessness. They may not look like it, but they are very spiritual creatures."

Then the image changed. William found himself looking at a panoply of faces, some smug, some projecting happiness, some trying to be glamorous, some totally inscrutable. A photo of an infamous dictator flashed past. An artist. A movie star. A business tycoon.

"On the other hand," said Proof, *"all of these people are evil."*

"But they look normal too." said William.

"And now maybe you understand what the banality of evil is."

William had never heard that word before.

"What's banality?" asked William.

"Ordinariness," said Proof.

"They do look ordinary," said William.

"Evil is a master of disguise. It pretends to be many things. Evil pretends to love. It pretends to help. It pretends to tell the truth. But it does none of those things. All it can do is mimic, distort and mock."

William watched the parallax playing out, studying the faces. He truly couldn't see anything evil about them, no unusual deformities, no jug ears, no scars, no Neanderthal brows. He thought about the people who boast that they can look into a person's eyes and determine moral character. That was impossible, since evil people hide in plain daylight.

"Fortunately, there is a way to identify evil," said Proof.

"How?"

"Look for the lies."

The faces on the parallax began to speak, their lips moving in ways small and large. Some with fierce hand gestures. Some defiant. Some ignoring criticisms.

"All those people are lying?" asked William.

"Nearly every minute of their lives. They don't even know that they're doing it. They're lost in their own matrix of deception. And we get lost in this matrix too, a labyrinth of never-ending deception. Then they look to impose their own lies upon other people."

He paused. *"Does the Ancient Engineer know that evil is in the system?"*

"Of course."

William watched the images flash past, one person after another. He imagined the lies coming out of their mouths.

"Can I ask another question?" William said.

"Of course."

"If the Ancient Engineer knows that evil is in the system, why doesn't he get rid of it?"

The entity known as Proof paused the parallax and turned his presence toward William. The two beings were facing one another in the void.

"He allows it to continue because of free will," said Proof.

William thought about that but hit a wall.

"That doesn't make any sense," he said.

"The universe is in a violent struggle," explained Proof. *"If humanity moves forward, it must be because it has overcome the force dragging it backward."*

William started to feel strange vibrations in his nonexistent body, as though the molecules of which he was composed were resisting this new environment. He ignored them and pressed on, hoping Proof wouldn't notice.

"*So we have to move toward selflessness, not selfishness,*" said William.

Proof responded, "*Lack of reflection. Plato called it the unexamined life.*"

William was finally able to put the Change Agent system into a bigger context.

"*And my team is part of this grand effort?*" he asked.

"*Your team,*" said Proof, "*is an attempt to advance all of humanity. Those who become CA3s have a powerful ripple effect. One spiritually advanced person can lead millions of people to the same spiritual advancement.*"

"*So why are you telling me this?*" asked William.

"*Because every coin has two sides. One evil person can create the same ripple effect, but for the worse,*" said Proof.

The long parallax winked on again. The screen showed scenes of mobs, violence, bizarre dictators, parents beating children, howling faces.

"*That's how millions of people lose their humanity. All it takes is one evil person in a position of power,*" said Proof.

As William watched the images, he felt the vibrations growing stronger. His vision, or whatever it was here, started to shake. The constellation became blurry. He looked back to Proof.

"*You didn't call me here just to discuss the nature of evil, did you?*" asked William.

"*Yes, I did,*" replied Proof.

"*Why?*" asked William.

Proof paused, as though weighing his words carefully. William felt the weight of a thousand things left unspoken. Then Proof's eyes landed on William.

"You're vibrating," said Proof.

"First tell me why you called me here," said William.

Proof's headlight eyes passed over William again, and he ignored the question.

"I have to send you back," said Proof.

"Tell me," said William.

"You can probably figure it out."

"It's Hunter. It has to be Hunter."

Proof didn't reply. Instead, his figure pulled away into the void and shrank into a small point of energy.

Then, without warning, the void twisted around William, spiraling like a sheet of black liquid swirling down a drain.

An instant later, William found himself standing in the corridor, the gate in front of him, the small light pulsing around the outside. He was back in his body.

Next to him, Shana was busy tapping away at the small screen. "Welcome back," she said, without looking up.

William blinked, spun around, then looked down at his body. He felt his arm. It was solid. "Wow. That felt like a snap minus a body."

"I wouldn't know," said Shana. "I've never been invited inside."

Her eyes flashed up at him, and he saw a bit of jealousy.

"Well," William said, "maybe he will someday."

"I wouldn't count on it. I'm just the help. You guys are the Change Agents."

William tried to lift her spirits. "We couldn't do any of this training without your help. You're essential."

Shana shrugged, appearing uncomfortable at the compliment. "You're too nice."

"But it's the truth."

Her shield went back up. "Have a good night, William."

The next morning, as William entered the galley, he saw four pairs of eyes tracking his entrance. The eyes belonged to his teammates.

"There he is," said Grace.

"We heard you met with Proof last night," said Hunter.

William smiled. "You people are horrible gossips."

"That's not a denial," said Jeremy.

"What did he tell you?" asked Trina.

Grace looked at him with eyebrows lifted. There was no hiding anything from his teammates, so William settled into a seat, his legs spread wide, his posture relaxed. "Well, it was kind of strange. We just talked about evil, mostly."

"What's his suite like?" asked Trina. "Is it totally tricked out?"

"It's empty," replied William.

"Empty like there's no furniture in it?" asked Jeremy.

"No, empty like there's nothing in it at all. I wasn't even there."

The team grew quiet. "So, where was your body?" asked Grace.

William shrugged. "I couldn't tell you. Maybe it was having a good time without me."

He looked around. "Did any of you see me doing anything weird last night?"

"Bro, that's pretty much every night," said Jeremy.

Sharp laughter from the team. The ice was broken just as quickly as it had formed. William didn't want the team to feel jealous that he'd been singled out for special attention. Their one-for-all-and-all-for-one attitude was the thing that would get them through to the next level. It needed to be preserved.

He wolfed down his breakfast, and a few minutes later the team members were climbing into their pods.

CHAPTER 21

S*NAP.*

William found himself balancing on the uppermost rung of a long ladder, one hand on the ladder, the other holding a trowel caked in what seemed to be wet mud.

Five hundred breaths.

He looked at his arm. His skin was an olive hue this time, definitely tanned, and on his face he could feel a moustache tickling his upper lip. On his chest was a loose white cotton garment spattered with bits of the gunk in his hand.

He was a laborer. That much was clear. He looked down. The ladder was at least forty feet high, and it was balanced on a scaffolding that was another thirty feet in the air. A group of men stood on the scaffolding below, and another group on the hard dirt below them. The men on the ground were carrying finished blocks of stone, one by one, and dropping them into a basket. A rope connected the basket to the scaffolding, and another one to William's level.

Next to him, another laborer was pulling finished stone blocks from another basket and arranging them in a geometric pattern. He was taking great care in the selection.

William glanced around. The two of them were working

on an enormous sheer wall. It seemed to be a religious structure.

Four hundred fifteen. Four hundred fourteen.

He watched his hand reach out and slap the gunk over the
most recent layer of stones on top of the wall and smooth it
out with the trowel. Then he heard himself grunt. To his
right, the other man grunted back, then whistled to the men
below.

The men began pulling on one end of the long rope, and
another basket slowly rose in the air toward William and his
colleague.

He felt himself wipe the sweat from his face on the shoulder of his garment. The sun was low in the sky but rising.
From this height, he could see the surrounding city. It was
packed with two and three-story buildings, some made of
stone, others of mud or rammed earth.

The second basket arrived. The men below shouted, and
suddenly the first basket dropped. William watched as the
other worker used his free hand to swing the new, full basket
around to take the first one's place.

Three hundred twenty-eight. Three hundred twenty-seven.

A nimbus appeared on the head of the man next to him. It
was yellow. That meant it was Trina. William wondered why
the nimbi seemed to lag behind the start of the snap. They
didn't appear for at least a hundred breaths.

"Hope you're not afraid of heights," communicated Trina.

"I don't want to chat," he replied. *"Let's focus on learning
how people make decisions."*

"So testy," she said.

They went about their work for the next few minutes, Trina stacking the blocks from the basket. William slathered the mortar over the top, filled in the spots between the blocks, and smoothed everything over.

Two hundred two. Two hundred one.

Trina's host leaned over to place a block on a distant ledge. The worker leaned out, one hand and foot on the ladder, the other hand and foot dangling out into space.

To William's horror, the ladder began to tip over.

"Ahhh!" shouted Trina's host.

William swung out into space, watched his hand reach over to the other ladder, and felt himself pull it back upright. Trina's host swung back to the safety of the ladder.

"How did you make that decision?" asked William.

"I'd prefer not to chat so much," she replied.

"So testy."

"It scared the crap out of me."

"I believe it."

The two workers stayed there for a while, perched near the tops of their ladders, waiting for the next load of blocks to be hoisted, enjoying the sun on their faces. William tried to discern the state of his host's mood, but it was hard to do. His host wasn't happy, or sad, or tired, or energetic. He just seemed emotionally switched off. William wondered if this was a typical state for humankind throughout its history. Or was it that sensitivity and empathy were more recent traits? Whatever the case, emptiness and lack of passion for life were evident.

One hundred forty-nine. One hundred forty-eight.

Suddenly William felt a creeping sensation on his host's spine. The man turned his head. Below the ladder, a strange creature was peering up at him from the ground. It was standing around the corner of the wall, so only its face and left arm were visible.

"*What is that?*" William said.

The creature slowly moved around the corner. It was vaguely human, with four limbs and a face, but that's where the similarity ended. Its skin was pale, a ghostly hue, and was covered in a series of small horns, like the stem of a rose. William couldn't see its face, but something about the creature felt menacing.

"*I don't know,*" Trina replied.

He watched it creep along the base of the structure. It moved like a jaguar or some other type of highly lethal cat. The creature lifted its head and looked up at William. Its eyes were two deep black gashes in its face.

"*William,*" it said.

William started to panic. This was a freakish creature, a thing of nightmares, and somehow it knew his name.

"*Trina, did you hear that?*" he said.

"*No.*"

"*It said my name.*"

The horned creature crept alongside the bottom of the wall to the base of the platform on which their ladders stood. The men on the platform scattered across the dirt, running, looking backward over their shoulders.

"*William, this is not good.*"

"*Stop talking so much. He can probably hear us.*"

The horned creature wrapped its pale fingers around the pilings supporting the scaffolding and began shaking them. The vibrations reached all the way up the scaffolding to the ladders, which William could feel swaying.

"William," the creature said.

"What do we do? We should do something," said Trina.

Now the creature had one hand on each piling and was standing between them like Samson, shaking both with all his might. It tilted its head back and let out a barbaric sound that made William's host's blood run cold.

Eighty-two. Eighty-one.

William felt the first piling start to give way. It was the one on the opposite side of the platform. Trina's ladder pitched to the side, away from him, and her host clung to the rungs, terrified.

"Get to the top of the wall!" said William.

"My host won't do it!" said Trina.

William felt himself climb two more rungs, swing himself off the ladder, and lower himself onto the top of the wall, one leg on each side. He felt the fresh mortar squish beneath his weight, the blocks resettle. This was the work that he and Trina had done not more than three minutes earlier, and it was nowhere near dry. If the blocks slid off the top of the wall, he'd slide with them.

"Influence him!" said William.

"I can't! He's too stubborn!" yelled Trina.

Trina's ladder pitched even farther. Her host was hanging half on and half off the ladder.

"Jump up here!" said William.

The pale, horned creature gave the pilings one final, massive shake, causing one to give way. The platform holding the ladders buckled and sank and collapsed. The three men who were standing on the platform screamed as they fell to the ground.

Next to William, Trina's ladder finally pitched over sideways. William watched in horror as Trina went falling, tumbling, screaming through the air, her nimbus growing smaller.

"*Trina*!" shouted William. "*No!*"

Forty-four. Forty-three.

He could feel the astonishment and disbelief of his host as Trina's host fell through the air sideways. Finally, she hit the ground, her shoulder and neck striking first. Her head crumpled beneath the weight of her body.

Her host lay there, unmoving, in the dirt seventy feet below William.

"*Trina!*" shouted William. "*Talk to me!*"

There was no response. The yellow nimbus was barely visible.

A sudden movement caught William's eye. Of the group of men who scattered, one had turned around. He was now running back *toward* the creature, his loose white garment flapping around him. William saw the man had a black nimbus around his head.

"*Hunter, what are you doing?*" shouted William. "*Get away from that thing!*"

Hunter ignored him. His host sprinted directly toward the bizarre creature and leapt onto its back.

"Aaaaaargh!" the man cried.

"Hunter, what are you doing?" shouted William.

As he watched, Hunter's host's body writhed and sizzled. Still, he stayed affixed to the creature's back, as though he were a piece of meat left cooking for so long that it had stuck to the grill. William heard the host's moans. He was in agony.

Then William saw something else. The black nimbus slowly disengaged from the man's head . . . and moved onto the creature's head. The creature blinked its demented eyes and then shook off the human from its back. The man fell backward onto the dirt and lay there, a field of red pinpricks forming a ghastly pattern on the front of his white garment.

The horned humanoid crept away from the man's body and then craned its blank face up the wall. It appeared to spot William and then, slowly, it began to climb the wall, as though it were a lizard.

It was heading toward William.

Twenty-three. Twenty-two.

William felt his host's blood run cold. There was nowhere to run, nowhere to hide, and even if there were, he felt the paralyzing fear in the man's hips and waist and torso.

Fifteen. Fourteen.

The horrific creature slowly scaled the wall, drawing ever closer to William, as though it had suction cups on its hands.

Nine. Eight.

William's hands frantically worked a block loose from the wall, one on top that hadn't dried yet. It popped free in his hands.

"Trina, where are you?"

Still no response. He peered down. Men had gather around Trina's host's body.

Five. Four.

The creature was almost within arm's reach now. William smelled its acrid, decayed presence. It was the scent of a creature that maybe was once human, but had gone horribly off course. Its black eyes were as flat as quarry holes. The tiny curved horns that covered its skin glinted beneath the noonday sun.

And the black nimbus was still affixed to its head.

"Hunter, get out of that thing!" William shouted, desperate now.

No response.

Three. Two.

The creature sprang at William. He lifted the block in self-defense, but it was too late. The humanoid was already on him, the small horns ripping into his flesh.

One.

William fell backward, the creature at his throat, falling through the air on the other side of the wall.

Snapback.

CHAPTER 22

SHANA HAD NO SOONER REMOVED THE TOP of the pod tank when William sprang out, the white spiritual-conductor goop still clinging to his back.

"Is Trina out yet?"

"No," said Shana, shocked, "I was going to her next. Why?"

He ripped off his cuff and ran over to Trina's pod. The digital display read 500 in red numerals. That meant she'd reached the end of her snap. William pressed a button, and the top of the pod tank slid open.

Trina lay there, unconscious.

"Trina, wake up," he said, trying to undo the medical cuff. "Her host was badly hurt, maybe even killed. She fell at least sixty or seventy feet."

"Let me handle it," said Shana, elbowing him aside. "I've been trained for these situations."

He stepped aside while Shana analyzed the girl's vital signs. She checked for respiration and then pulled a small radio from her pocket and spoke urgently into it. "Proof, we have a medical situation."

There was a small knocking from Jeremy's pod. Shana glanced over. "Would you let him out? And the others too?"

William ran over to Jeremy's pod and slid open the top. His teammate took a look at his face and stifled a laugh. "Well, Shana, you've gotten a lot uglier."

"I'm not in the mood," William said. He removed the medical cuff and offered Jeremy a hand, pulling him out. "Trina's in trouble, man."

Jeremy's face darkened. "What happened?"

"Her host fell off a ladder. About seventy feet."

"Are you serious?" asked Jeremy.

"Yes." William went to Hunter's pod and slid open the lid. His teammate was already scowling at him. "Oh, it's you."

"What the hell, Hunter? Didn't you hear me in the snap?"

Hunter sat up and removed his cuff. "No, I didn't."

"Your host jumped onto that bizarre creature, and your nimbus was transferred onto it."

Hunter made a pantomime of thinking. "Hmm. I didn't notice that an unholy creature leapt onto my body and tried to suck out my soul. Nope, just overlooked it."

William shot him an assassin's look. "We'll talk about it later. We've got a problem over here."

At that moment, Proof appeared in the doorway and went to Trina's pod and took a long searching look at her condition. "Hold on," he said.

The team watched as their coach went to a closet, pulled out a device, scanned it over Trina's body, and then waited. William had no clue what the device could be. Evidently, it was important, because when Proof looked at the readout, his face fell.

"Oh boy." He turned to Shana. "Is the medical bay ready?"

"Yes, it is." said Shana.

"Run and make sure the doors are open." He turned to Jeremy and Hunter. "I need both of you to assist me. Come on."

Jeremy sped over. Hunter followed reluctantly.

Meanwhile, William realized that he hadn't opened Grace's pod. He went over to it, popped it open, and undid her cuff. Grace sat up on her hands and watched the three pull the unconscious Trina out of her pod and carry her out of the room.

Grace looked up at William. "What happened to her?"

William was as white as a ghost. "Everybody's worst nightmare."

A bit later, the debriefing room was abuzz with conversation, which was normal. This time, however, it contained only four team members, not five. Trina's customary seat was empty.

Proof stood before them, his hands held up in a calming gesture.

"She's resting in the medical bay," he said, "and *you* can rest assured that she's doing fine."

Jeremy raised his hand. "Repeat what happened again, because I don't really believe it."

"She fell seventy feet in her host's body," said William. "It happened right next to me."

"But *her* body is damaged?" said Jeremy. "Her actual body here?"

"Yes," said Proof.

"What exactly is the injury?"

"We're looking into that right now," said Proof. They all glanced over at Shana's customary chair, which was again empty.

Hunter kicked the chair in front of him, and it skittered a few feet across the floor. It was a pointless act of symbolic cruelty, and his eyes were full of anger.

"What is your problem?" asked Jeremy.

"Proof said that nothing that happened in a snap would affect us," said Hunter.

"Physically," added Grace.

Proof bit on his lower lip and nodded. "True, we did say that. And we said it because nothing had ever happened to any of you. But there's a first time for everything. It seems you aren't totally immune to injuries sustained by your hosts."

Grace raised her hand. "What exactly happened? Why did her host fall?"

All eyes looked at William. He was tired of telling the story but began to explain again. "My host and her host were working next to one another, on top of a wall. There was this really weird creature that attacked us. It shook the platform that our ladders were on. My host escaped by climbing onto the top of the wall. Hers didn't, and she fell."

Proof came around the table and stood close to William. "What kind of creature was this?"

"It's hard to describe," replied William.

"Was it human?" asked Proof.

William scrunched up his face, trying to describe it. "I don't know. I'd call it humanoid. It had the shape of a human but was all pale. And the skin had little . . . horns sprouting out." He held his raised fingers against his arm to illustrate the look of the horns.

Proof grew still. "Small horns?"

"Yes."

"Was it wearing clothing?"

"No. It seemed alien."

William suddenly became aware of how closely the others were listening to him.

"Creepy," said Jeremy.

"Do you remember anything else about it?" asked Grace.

"Yeah," William said. "It could climb walls. But Hunter would probably know more. His host jumped on the thing."

All eyes turned to Hunter. He shrugged and nonchalantly said, "William was a little too scared and must've been seeing things. My host never touched that thing."

William felt the rage building inside him. "Hunter, I *saw* your nimbus float onto the creature's head."

Hunter raised his voice in response. "You were damn near scared to death on top of a ladder with a bizarre creature crawling toward you! You think we believe your eyewitness account?"

Before he could answer, Proof said, "Wait, is that true? This creature could crawl up a wall?"

William put aside his anger with Hunter. "Yeah. It just came up the wall toward me, seventy feet straight up, crawling like a spider. Then it leaped on me a second before the snapback."

"What did it feel like?" asked Proof.

William heard the word come out of his mouth. "*Evil.*"

He was just as surprised as everybody else that he'd said it. Jeremy and Grace looked stricken. Hunter regarded him with tight lips, his fingers working as though rolling small bits of paper.

"How could you tell that it was evil?" said Proof.

The teacher caught William's eye, and in his look was a challenge. This had been the subject of their conversation the day before, when he'd been invited into Proof's so-called private quarters.

"Because it didn't have any self-awareness," said William, looking at Hunter. "It felt like a shark, moving through the sea, eating anything it could find."

"And it killed humans?" asked Proof.

"Probably Trina's host."

Proof circled around toward his podium. He looked uncharacteristically angry. "I know what you saw."

"What?"

"It's an old entity. It has many names, but one of them is Little Horn."

William nodded. He could understand how it had earned that nickname.

"How long has it been around?" asked Jeremy.

Proof shrugged. "I don't know. Only the Ancient Engineer knows."

"Where does it come from?" asked Trina.

"From the days of old, before time," he replied.

"Have you ever encountered it?" asked William.

Proof looked distraught. "In a different form, yes. It takes on many disguises."

William said, "So do you think that this thing was trying to kill our hosts?"

"No," said Proof. "I think it was trying to kill *you*."

William stood up and walked to the back of the room, his hands over his eyes. Everyone fell silent again, deferring to him. He couldn't talk. He couldn't think. He couldn't even see normally. It isn't every day you're informed that an ancient evil creature has targeted you for special treatment.

"Urp," said Hunter, an attempt at humor. It fell flat.

Jeremy rubbed his forehead. "So explain why this thing is targeting us?"

"Because your spiritual awareness is growing," said Proof. He took a deep breath before continuing. "Your spirit, everyone's spirit, acts like a beacon. Imagine a lighthouse suddenly turning on one night. If it's strong enough, all sorts of creatures in the vicinity see it, and are drawn to it. Proud and noble creatures, vicious and small creatures, and bizarre creepy-crawlies."

Proof swept a finger across the room. "You are *all* going to have to deal with this problem from now on. Entities of all kinds will be drawn to you, and you can't control who they are. Some will be very good, and they will help you. Some will be really bad, and they will be your enemies. Some, like Little Horn, will not even be totally human, and they will destroy you if they can."

There was silence for a moment while the four team members took in that news. Finally Jeremy cleared his throat. "You said that we had three snaps left. If Trina was so close to her host that she actually picked up his physical injury, this must mean that we're getting closer to CA3."

Proof looked like he wanted to say more, but he murmured only, "It's really up to the Ancient Engineer."

"Give us a clue," said Hunter.

"I truly can't. I'm just here to help you find your own path. The decision is ultimately up to you."

The door opened, and Shana poked her head in. Everybody turned around. "Sorry to interrupt, but Trina is awake. You told me to let you know."

"All right, team," Proof said, "I'm going to sit with her for a while. Remember, the Ancient Engineer . . . "

"Loves us and wants us to succeed," all four said.

Proof looked at them searchingly. "You are all getting really tired of saying that, aren't you?"

"Yes," said Hunter, rolling his eyes.

Proof regarded him with wise but tired eyes. "Someday you'll understand how true it is."

CHAPTER 23

A FEW HOURS LATER, WHEN WILLIAM learned that Trina had been released from the medical bay, he ran to the living area.

He arrived to find her sitting on one of the low sofas, propped up by pillows. She was wearing a loose yellow shift. Her face was pale and dazed, and the light in her eyes seemed to have dimmed. The other three team members were already there, Jeremy next to her, and Grace holding her hand. Hunter was on the other side of the room, with his arms crossed.

"You made it," said William, approaching her.

Trina managed a half-smile. He sat down cross-legged in front of the chair. "I thought you were dead."

"I'm not," she said, "but I think my host died."

"What did it feel like?" asked Grace.

Trina grew dazed for a moment. "It was weird. It felt like someone was enveloping me and swallowing me whole."

"That wasn't death," Hunter said. His voice was harsh. "That was something else. Death feels different. It feels like running down a long tunnel toward total freedom."

"How do you know?" asked Jeremy.

"Because I remember dying once."

That took the team aback. All five of them knew that

they'd experienced other people's lives, and they knew that they had faint memories from those lives that, if jogged properly, they could remember. They'd even sat around this very room, joking about it, after several of the snaps. But none of them remembered the actual deaths.

"You never told us that before," said William.

"You never asked," he replied.

They were all facing Hunter now. Jeremy said, "But Proof asked us if we had ever died in a snap. You said no."

Hunter shrugged. "I lied."

William felt anger, frustration and a hundred other negative emotions. Lately, Hunter had become a black hole of attention and negativity. He flouted rules and disrespected the rest of the team. There didn't seem to be any way to win with him. He would always win, because there was no bottom to his behavior. He was unable to feel shame.

Grace waved her hand and broke the awkwardness in the air. "Can we get back to Trina?"

"Yes, let's," said William, glad for the change of subject.

"Proof told us that we didn't have to worry if our host died," said Grace.

"He said that we only had to worry if the host stopped breathing," said Jeremy.

William nodded. He remembered Proof explaining that the only criterion determining the length of a tag-along was five hundred breaths. They'd presumed that if a host died before that, Proof would intervene and manually pull the team member back to the pod tank.

Trina looked pensive. "I'm not sure that the host died."

"You said that it felt like someone was enveloping you and swallowing you," said Jeremy.

"Yes."

"William told us about that strange creature. Could it have been because of that?"

"Maybe," Trina said.

She looked slightly dazed and turned to William. "You saw it too?"

He nodded. "At the debriefing, Proof said it's an ancient entity called Little Horn."

Trina looked distant, as though remembering something. Then she blanched slightly. "It felt like he was possessing me and the host. It was, I don't know . . . suffocating our souls."

The group fell silent. William sat there, regarding Trina for a little bit longer. Then he looked over at Hunter, who had found a pad of paper and was absentmindedly drawing dark rings on the paper.

"Hunter," he heard himself say, "do you want to be part of this team?"

"Why do you ask, William?" He spit out the last word as though spitting out a bitter cherry pit.

"Because we're not really sure. Whose side are you on, the team's or your own?"

Hunter sneered. "Well, since the team is the only way that I can improve myself, then I'd have to say that I'm on the side of the team. Wouldn't you say that too, William?"

William got to his feet. "See, it's that kind of response that makes us doubt you. *I'm part of the team because I have to be.* We're all counting on you, Hunter."

Hunter got to his feet. "You can depend on me, William." A facsimile of sincerity appeared on his face.

"I don't think we can," said William.

"Guys," Jeremy said as he stood up, "we're all in this together."

"Exactly my point," said William. "We're all in this together, Hunter."

Hunter drew closer, flexing his arm, nostrils flaring slightly. William clenched his fists and assumed a wide stance. This was going to be a fight, a real fight, a long overdue one, and everybody in the room knew it.

Jeremy inserted himself between them. "Guys."

"Get out of the way!" said Hunter.

"No," said Jeremy, "I'm not going to let you do this!"

A spasm of rage passed across Hunter's face. A strange roar erupted from his throat, and he took Jeremy by the shoulders and threw him across the living area. Jeremy stumbled, his thin arms windmilling, and crashed into a wall. He collapsed to the floor.

Now Hunter faced William, his eyes full of manic intensity. William felt his resolve start to falter. Maybe he shouldn't have picked this fight.

"Hunter!" said a stern voice, "stand down."

Everybody turned. Proof stood in the doorway of the living area. He wore a stern look on his face, and his hands were placed firmly on his hips.

Hunter lowered his head, averted his eyes, and slunk away toward the corner of the room, opposite from where Jeremy lay on the floor. Grace ran over to Jeremy, while Trina looked like she wanted to cry.

"What just happened in here?" asked Proof.

Grace helped Jeremy roll over onto his back "Hunter threw Jeremy across the room, and it looks like he smashed his head into the wall." To Jeremy she said, "Are you okay? Can you hear me?"

Jeremy blinked. Then he touched his forehead and winced. "I can hear you fine. But my head, I don't know."

"He's going to need to go the medical bay too," said Grace. "At least so we can check for a concussion."

Shana appeared behind Proof. "I heard something crash in here."

"It was Jeremy," said Proof. "Go help him."

Shana knelt down next to Jeremy. Proof turned his attention to Hunter. "What would cause you to physically attack a member of your own team?"

"He was getting in my way," said Hunter, his voice rising, as though he were in agony. As William watched, it appeared that Hunter had taken on the mannerisms of a small child.

"What was Jeremy trying to do?"

Trina interrupted. "He was trying to keep Hunter and William from getting into a fight."

"I don't think that Hunter is working for the team," William said.

Proof's eyes searched William's face for signs of deception. "So you're saying you don't trust him?"

"I don't." said William.

"Would you like to be able to trust him?"

"Yes, I would."

Proof turned to Hunter. "Would you like to earn William's trust?"

Hunter crossed his arms and looked physically uncomfortable. "Sure."

"Is that a yes?"

"Sure."

Proof repeated the question. "*Is that a yes?*"

Hunter rolled his eyes. "Yes."

The team's coach nodded, and then turned around to address everybody. "So here's what's going to happen. Tomorrow will be a special tag-along for only Hunter and William. The two of them will use this opportunity to learn to trust one another."

"So we won't get in the pods tomorrow?" asked Trina.

"You definitely weren't going to anyway, and now neither is Jeremy."

"What about me?" asked Grace.

"Sit this one out." Proof pointed at Hunter and William with each hand. "Only you two. Tomorrow, both of you learn to get along, or else the team won't advance."

Proof left, and as soon as he was out of sight, William walked back to his own room, fuming. *He* wasn't the one with the personality problem; Hunter was. But now it was going to be on his shoulders to mend the relationship. That wasn't fair. Proof knew about Hunter's antisocial personality traits.

As he climbed into bed that night, William realized that his relationship with Hunter was in fact as much of a test as the snaps were. And it was up to him to make the relationship work.

CHAPTER 24

NOBODY SPOKE AT BREAKFAST IN THE
galley the next morning. Jeremy had a bandage
across the side of his head and was picking at a
plate of runny scrambled eggs. Trina was sipping a mug of tea,
still looking out of sorts. Grace was finishing her usual yogurt.

William looked down at his customary breakfast, but he
didn't have much of an appetite. He felt as though he was
about to enter a boxing ring. Except, unlike a boxing match,
where his job would be to knock out his opponent, his task
here was to make peace with him. He imagined that he had a
better chance of doing that while they were both in other
people's bodies.

That opponent was Hunter. He hadn't shown up to
breakfast yet. William had seated himself facing the door, so
he could see his rival's arrival. Truth be told, he didn't feel
comfortable turning his back on Hunter, not after yesterday's attack on Jeremy.

"Are you ready?" asked Jeremy.

William screwed up his face. "I don't know. Making peace
with Hunter in a snap isn't going to be easy."

"We were talking last night," said Grace, indicating Trina

with her eyes, "and we think Proof is testing him. Not you."

"For what?"

"For empathy."

William chewed on the last piece of bacon, thinking. "You could be right."

"I mean, did you see how fast Proof was at the door, and how fast he decided how to resolve the situation?" said Grace.

"Yeah, it seemed a little too quick," replied William.

Jeremy interrupted. "I bet he's been thinking about a way to test Hunter for a long time. We just gave him the excuse he needed to implement it."

"You're the guinea pig," said Trina, smiling faintly.

"Well," said William, rising to his feet, "some people eat guinea pigs."

He carried his plate to the sink and left the galley. "Good luck," Jeremy said as he was leaving.

William went back to his room, washed his hands and face in the sink, and then looked at himself in the mirror. "It comes down to this."

He went back down the corridor to the pod tank. Shana was already there, as was Proof, waiting. They both stood up as he entered. "Hey," he said.

"As soon as Hunter shows up, we can get started," Shana said.

"He wasn't at breakfast."

She and Proof exchanged looks. "I'll go get him," Shana said.

No sooner had she taken one step towards the door when Hunter burst into the room. His eyes were alive with energy, and his entire body seemed animated. "Sorry," said Hunter, "I was busy."

"As long as you got here," said Proof.

"William," said Hunter, approaching him with an extended hand, "I'm sorry about yesterday. Let's make it up here."

William looked at his hand suspiciously. Then he looked up at Hunter's eyes. There was no malice in them, nothing except directness and forthrightness. Then William remembered what Proof had said to him about evil people being masters of disguise, leading lives of lies.

Reluctantly he grasped Hunter's hand and shook it. The hand felt strong and well formed.

They released the grasp, and both turned toward Proof, who said, "This snap is a little different because you won't be selecting anything. I've made the selection already."

"Sounds good to me," said Hunter, clapping his hands together. "Let's do this! Ready, William?"

William kept his eyes focused on Proof. "Yes I am, Hunter."

Proof gestured to a pair of pods. "Please enter."

William noticed that they'd been arranged side by side.

William climbed into one and lay back; Hunter did the same in the other. Shana came to William's side and affixed the cuff. "Good luck on this one," she said.

There was a note of warning in her voice. William's eyes found hers. "Why do I need luck?"

"I just have a funny feeling," she whispered.

She lowered the top of the pod, and a moment later William felt everything go dark. He waited for the parallax to arrive above, but this time there was only a single image.

CHAPTER 25

S *NAP.*

William found himself lying on a gurney. He was wearing a tiny patterned hospital gown.

Five hundred breaths.

A huge pain was ripping through his chest. His fingers clenched and unclenched, and his gown was soaked in sweat. A beeping monitor to his left told him that things were not all right.

His host was very ill.

The hospital room was modern. A flat-screen television on the wall ahead of him showed a talking head on CNN describing a terrorist attack somewhere in the Middle East. He was in the contemporary era, that much was clear. It was a welcome change from the usual dirt villages and horrific scenes of slaughter that they'd snapped to before.

This suffering, however, had simply taken a different form. William had never known sickness, and judging from the strange, swelling feeling in his body, he wished that he never had. He'd much rather take his chances with a snake or a hippo, not a battalion of tiny, invisible germs. There was no way to combat that, nothing he could do except lie here and wait.

He turned his head. Sitting next to him was a woman, presumably his wife. She was ordinary looking, with brown hair, a simple top, and eyes reddened from crying or fatigue or both.

"Baby," she said.

"Yeah," he replied. His voice was a croak.

"The doctor just gave us some great news. Your vitals are coming back."

He felt himself swell with a little bit of hope. "Which ones?"

"All of them, baby." She wiped a tear away. "Heart rate, respiration, white blood cells, everything."

"I'm getting better." William heard himself say the words, mostly as a reassurance.

His host's wife gripped his hand. It felt hot and alive compared to his. "We always knew you would come back. Even when you hit bottom last week, I knew you would. Your spirit is so strong."

He looked around the room. "Where's Kristin?"

"She went to find a sandwich."

Four hundred forty-six. Four hundred forty-five.

William settled his head back into the pillow and looked at the ceiling. "I bet I'm prettier than she is right now."

"Do you want to see yourself, baby?"

William perked up. In all of these snaps, never once had he looked into a mirror. The snaps usually didn't last long enough, and most of the locations were places where mirrors were luxury items.

"I'll probably regret it," he said.

"No," she replied, "all things considered, you don't look so bad." His wife reached into her purse and pulled out her compact and opened it and held the mirror up to his face.

William looked in the mirror. He saw a pasty-faced middle-aged man with no hair, no eyebrows, no eyelashes. He had a bit too much fat around the jowls, and his skin had a yellowish tint that was definitely not healthy. He looked like the definition of a struggling hospital patient.

It took William aback, seeing a different face from his in the reflection. After all, it was a primitive thing, seeing one's face, and so this experience was deeply unsettling. He gestured for her to lower the mirror.

"Not bad, huh?" she said.

"I guess," he said. His throat suddenly felt dry, and it occurred to him that he needed some water. He made a few gasping noises with his throat.

"Water? Here you go."

His wife lifted a small cup of water to his lips, and he felt the cool liquid hit his mouth. It ran down his throat, soothing him along the way.

The door handle turned, and a doctor entered the room. He was Indian, fairly short, and he wore a white lab coat.

Three hundred eighty. Three hundred seventy-nine.

"Good afternoon, Mr. Daniels," he said, looking at his clipboard. "How are you feeling today?"

Mr. Daniels. William had never heard a host's name before, at least not in English.

"Better, I guess," William replied, his voice scratchy.

The doctor studied him for a moment. "I appreciate your optimism," he said. "A positive attitude has been shown to correlate with positive outcomes. However, I've been studying your charts, and there's still quite a bit of cause for concern."

William felt his host's spirits begin to fall. A heat started in his cheeks and spread to the back of his head and down his back. He felt a buzzing anxiety in his thighs. Sweat sprang out on his palms.

Meanwhile, his wife got to her feet and was wringing her hands anxiously. "But Dr. Linder informed us yesterday that everything was improving."

The Indian doctor lifted his hand up, and she quieted. "I spoke with Dr. Linder this morning about your husband's case, and after further review he does regret that feedback. The fact is that your husband is not out of the woods, not even close. In fact, we are worried about total system collapse."

William's wife let out a shriek. William rolled his eyes up to the ceiling, wishing desperately he could be out of this body, out of this snap, back to himself.

"Doctor, what is wrong with me this time?" he heard himself say.

"Brain tumors are tricky things," said the doctor. "They affect people in different ways. As they move and grow, they press upon different parts of the body."

He went on to a disquisition describing William's host's case. He had something called a Glioblastoma, and it came with an average life expectancy of fourteen months. He was receiving Temozolomide as a part of chemotherapy.

"So are you worried that it could be spreading?" said his wife.

"Potentially. We'll know more when the radiologist looks at the scan shortly." He mustered a smile. "I'll be back."

The doctor nodded and left the room.

William's wife sat in a chair, made a fist, and laid her forehead upon it. She began to cry.

"Sweetheart," he croaked.

"Not right now," she said. "I just can't. It's just, no, I can't."

She left the room with her hand over her face, the door closing behind her. William knew that she was crying and that she didn't want him to see her doing so.

Two hundred two. Two hundred one.

The talking heads on television were chatting about six more weeks of winter, the caption read something about Punxsutawney Phil. William watched his hand pick up the remote control and press the big red power button. The screen went black.

His host wasn't going to make it. He could tell.

William began to think about mortality. His host was going to die, like all of us, but this guy Daniels was going to die sooner rather than later. He felt his host come to an understanding of that, an acceptance, and immediately a sense of calm settled over his body and soul like a soft blanket on a colicky baby. He had faith in something beyond himself, and that's where his piece came from.

"*It's okay,*" said William to his host.

He'd never done that before, making direct communication with a host. Truth be told, William hadn't even known until just now that he could do such a thing. But the time seemed right. Daniels grew very still. William could tell he was listening.

"*You'll continue your existence later, somewhere else.*"

William realized he was having the conversation that people have with spirits before they die, only he was on the other side, playing the part of the spirit.

"*I've had a good life*," Daniels said.

"*Then count yourself blessed.*"

"*My wife and daughter don't deserve to be alone.*"

"*They won't be. There are billions of people all around them.*"

"*It feels like you're right here with me.*"

William fought the urge to tell the truth. "*I am, but I have to leave soon.*"

The door to the hospital room flew open. It was the Indian doctor again, followed by Daniels' wife, followed by a girl who he presumed was Daniels' daughter. She was in that awkward stage of growth that ten-year-old girls sometimes find themselves in, a mess of gangly limbs. Behind the three of them were two nurses.

"Doctor, that is *absurd*!" his wife was saying.

"The results show that total system breakdown is imminent," the doctor said.

One hundred thirty-nine. One hundred thirty-eight.

"I demand to speak to another specialist," she said fiercely.

"You're welcome to do that while we're sedating and intubating your husband."

"No," she said, "putting him on that thing is ridiculous. He can breathe, and talk, on his own, right now."

The doctor turned to face her, calm. "Mrs. Daniels, this is a precaution for what may be arriving shortly. It's better to handle it now, when there's no urgency, than later, when there is."

William felt his host grow petrified with fear. "What are you going to do?" Daniels asked.

The Indian doctor came over to the side of the bed and stood over him. He looked down with compassion and competence. "We're going to put you on a ventilator," he said.

Panic wriggled through his host's body. William had never felt anything like that before. "I'm breathing fine."

"You might not be tomorrow."

"Then wait until tomorrow."

"No," he said, "we have to do it right now. The respiratory therapist is already here, and she's going to take you down to the ICU."

William heard himself whimper.

The Indian doctor laid a hand upon his arm. "Please, William, it's for your own good."

His host looked up at the doctor. "My name is Kenneth."

The doctor shook his head as though he'd made a mistake. "Sorry, I don't know why I just said that. Your name is Kenneth."

"Why did you call me William?"

The doctor shrugged. "It was just a slip of the tongue."

William looked at the doctor. As they held one another's eyes, he saw a dark mass slowly form around the doctor's head. It was a nimbus, a black one.

That wasn't just any doctor.

It was Hunter.

And his host was placing William's host on a ventilator, a machine that did the breathing for a person.

In other words, William's host wouldn't be taking any more breaths. Then it suddenly hit him: This was sabotage.

Eighty-three. Eighty-two.

The nurses arrived on either side of the bed, lifted the brakes, and rolled William's host, Kenneth Daniels, out of the room.

"Kenneth, I'm going to take over your body."

"What?"

"Just go along with it."

William exerted his newfound influence, and sure enough, he felt himself in total control. Immediately, he tried to roll out of the gurney. When the nurses saw what he was doing, one of them restrained him by placing her arm across his chest.

"I want to leave!" William shouted. Those were his words, not Kenneth's.

"You're going to be ventilated," said the nurse who was holding him down. She lifted a radio to her face. "Code one sixty-nine, south elevators. Code one sixty-nine, destination ICU."

William attempted to throw himself off the gurney, but his host's body was so weak that he merely slumped over.

"Can you keep an eye on him?" said one nurse.

"I'm trying!" said the other.

At the elevators, two male nurses were waiting, one holding a pair of plastic straps. Before William knew it, they'd tied his arms to the gurney. He lay back and shut his eyes. Then he opened them and said, "That doctor is trying to kill me."

"Who?" said one of the nurses. William could tell he was trying not to laugh.

"The Indian one."

"Dr. Kamil is a well-respected member of our medical community."

"Maybe," said William, "but there's someone inside of him, a bad force named Hunter, who's trying to get me. I don't know how to say it, like, *spiritually suspended*. Do you understand?"

The elevator doors opened. The male nurses glanced at each other knowingly. "Sure, that's right. Dr. Kamil is possessed by a devil."

Fifty-two. Fifty-one.

"No," said William, "stop making fun of me. I'm serious! You're looking at me. What's my name. I can't remem . . . wait. It's Kenneth, Kenneth Daniels, right? And that's who my body is, yeah, but the person speaking to you right now is actually someone else! *My* name, this man inside Kenneth Daniels, is William, and I'm part of a team of Change Agents who are trying to reach Level Three, because that's how the world ultimately advances and comes to a higher understanding. But this guy Hunter doesn't want us to do it! He doesn't want us to do it! He's corrupt!"

The elevator went down three floors while he was talking, and all four nurses looked straight ahead, smiles turning the corners of their mouths.

"This isn't a joke!" said William, frantic now. "I'm serious! We have been sent here to temporarily occupy people's bodies and learn from them, learn empathy, learn whatever helps our spiritual development! We get five hundred breaths in each person. I'm almost done with this body, but Hunter, inside Dr. Kamil, is trying to sabotage me!"

The doors opened, and the nurses pushed him along the corridor into an empty room. The respiratory therapist was already there, tracheotomy tube in hand.

"Don't do this!" William shouted.

Twenty-three. Twenty-two.

"Mr. Daniels, this is for your own good," said a nurse.

"No, it's for William's *bad*!" he shouted. "Kenneth Daniels doesn't need a ventilator! Dr. Kamil is trying to *sabotage* me!"

Then it hit William like a ton of bricks. *I need to speed my breathing up and get the five hundred before they put me on a ventilator.* Frantically he began to grasp each breath as quickly as possible.

"Slow down that breathing, Mr. Daniels," said a nurse.

William's cheeks puffed in and out, in and out.

Sixteen. Fifteen.

One of the male nurses gripped William's host's forearm while the other one arrived with a needle. The tip broke through the skin and plunged into the blood vessel. William felt the sedative hit him, and suddenly the urgency disappeared. His body went limp. His eyelids grew heavy. His heartbeat slowed.

Nine. Eight.

"Janine, you want to do it now?" asked a nurse.

"No," came the response, "Dr. Kamil wants to be present. We wait."

Their voices drifted into murmurs as the sedative spread through William's host's body. His eyes blurred, lost focus. He lost the ability to speak. His breathing slowed.

Six. Five.

A blurry brown figure in a white coat arrived. It was Dr. Kamil.

"He's been muttering about people living inside him," said a nurse.

"He said there's a devil inside you," said another.

"Poor guy," replied Dr. Kamil. "That tumor is really doing a number on his cognition. All right, Janine, proceed."

William felt his host's body prepped, prodded, and poked. Tape on his face. Then suddenly the taste of plastic running down his throat, deep, deep into his chest.

Three. Two.

The final inhale stuck in the host's throat as the machine took over. One more breath to go, but he was no longer breathing on his own.

This meant one thing. There would be no snapback.

William was suspended at four hundred ninety-nine breaths.

CHAPTER 26

HOURS LATER, WILLIAM SWAM UP TO the surface of consciousness and tried to break through. He could feel that he was still in Kenneth's body, that he was still in the hospital's ICU, and that he wasn't breathing. But his host's perceptions were smeared and blurry, and even his thought processes were slow and disjointed.

He tried to open his eyes, but they wouldn't crack more than a quarter open. He tried to lift a hand, but it was like pushing against a concrete wall. He even tried to speak, and that's when he felt it.

The ventilator tube.

The plastic thing that had been shoved in his mouth and down his throat. It was still there. It'd been affixed there with tape and some sort of mask. He felt it pushing air into his lungs and then pulling out the carbon dioxide, in a slow rhythm. *In, out. In, out.*

This was his existence now. Trapped inside a sedated body that was no longer breathing on its own. Paused at breath number four hundred ninety-nine, unable to complete the snap. He wanted to scream and so did his host, but he couldn't.

Then he thought about Hunter, and he grew even more angry.

They'd been sent to this snap by Proof. The goal was for them to learn to trust each other. The implied meaning, at least to William, was that Hunter had better take the opportunity to build a better relationship with William.

Instead, he took over Dr. Kamil so that the Indian doctor would do his bidding. It was a strange decision. William's host's wife had even been talking about how good her husband's numbers had been, how he'd been improving. And then Dr. Kamil entered, changed the interpretation, gave a bogus diagnosis, and forced William's host onto a ventilator.

But why? That was the million-dollar question. The only answer that William could come up with was cruelty. Hunter was not just avoiding building trust. He had been purposefully trying to *hurt* William by keeping him suspended inside his sick host. Being on a ventilator wasn't risk free either, so poor Kenneth Daniels was also suffering from Hunter's actions, in addition to having cancer.

William felt the rage gathering inside him. Not just for himself, but for this poor host who now had to endure even more.

He saw two nurses enter the room. "How's Mr. Daniels doing this morning? Good!"

William grew frustrated. That nurse knew good and well that he couldn't respond. Suddenly he felt a cough rack his body.

"Uh oh," said the nurse. "That doesn't sound good. You should know that your risk of pneumonia is going to go up as long as you're on this thing, so let's keep you healthy."

She put on sterile gloves and grabbed some antiseptic wipes from the counter and approached his face. She studied it. "Well, your eyes are open, pupils are responsive. I'd say the sedative wore off. Now, I'm just going to clean the tube so those nasty little bacteria don't get in your body."

He felt the cold antiseptic wipe swabbing the plastic around his lips, even inside his mouth.

"There," she said, stepping back. "Now, do you have to go to the bathroom? Lift one finger for yes."

William felt his host lift one finger. It was true; his bladder was fairly full.

"All right, let's see what we can do about that."

Ten minutes later, the catheter had been inserted into his host's male member, and the urine was being drained away. William felt even more incapacitated now. This was sheer torture.

"Would you like the television on?"

William felt his throat working itself, a useless exercise. Kenneth really wanted to speak, tube be damned.

"What was that?" asked the nurse.

He pointed to the ring finger on his left hand.

"Ah, your wife," said the nurse. "She'll be allowed in later. We want to keep the environment sterile for as long as possible, okay? Now, would you like the television on? Lift one finger for yes."

William watched his finger go up.

The nurse switched on the flat-screen television and put on the news again. "I'm going to leave the remote here, next to your finger. I'll check back in on you soon."

She left the room, and William was alone, still strapped to the gurney, a plastic tube down his throat, a television playing silently, and a sense of incredible injustice growing within him.

Hunter had not only managed to avoid building trust, he'd flat-out lied to, manipulated and hurt William. If this tag-along ever managed to end, he swore to take his revenge on Hunter.

William lay there, stewing in his own anger, while the images flickered across the screen. Then his host fell unconscious once more.

Twelve hours later, his eyelids fluttered awake. Night had fallen, darkness outside the window. The television was turned off. Next to him, the ventilator machine hummed. The plastic was still in his mouth.

"*Kenneth,*" William said.

"*Oh God, why are you still with me?*"

"*I'm supposed to leave, but I need you to take one more breath.*"

"*I swear I'm going crazy,*" said his host. "*They already think I'm crazy because of everything you made me say.*"

"*You're not.*"

"*Who are you again? Some kind of angel?*"

"My name is William, and it's hard to explain."

"Please God help me. Stop talking to me inside my head. Leave me alone," said Kenneth.

"Take one more breath, and I will," replied William.

"I'd have to remove the tube. I can't do that."

William knew that was the only solution. *"Kenneth, you don't need the ventilator. That doctor was trying to hurt me."*

"By punishing me?"

"It's complicated. I'm sorry. But can you take out the tube, even just for one breath?"

"My hands are tied."

William looked to the right. The IV stand had a long hook branching out from it. *"Try to hook the tube on the IV stand."*

"All right."

William felt his host lean over, snag the tube on the branch, then pull down hard with his neck. It didn't budge.

"I think they taped it on my face."

"Try again," said William.

His host leaned over and pulled down even harder. This time, the IV stand came crashing down to the floor. The tube was still hooked on the stand, and it pulled his host's body down with it.

Now William felt himself hanging part-way off the gurney, his hands still strapped to the rails, but his upper body being tugged down to the floor.

"Oh God, this hurts," said Kenneth.

"I know. I feel it too."

"Get out of me."

"*That's what I'm trying to do.*"

"*What is it you want?*"

"*I was sent here to try to learn what it's like to be someone else.*"

"*Now you know. Leave me.*"

William stopped talking. His presence seemed to be a torture for the man, and the relationship wasn't going anywhere.

The minutes stretched into hours, day turned to night and back to day, and William's host's condition remained exactly the same. The man's wife spent most of the time at his side, looking wrung out.

William listened to the sound, in and out, of the ventilator, trying to figure out how to remove the tube from his throat. He entertained fantasies of pain-inducing ways to get back at Hunter. He thought about Grace, Jeremy, Trina, hoping they were all okay. He wondered what was happening back in the pod tank.

"*William,*" said Kenneth.

That jolted him back to awareness. His host was communicating with him. That was unusual, and it meant that his host had already developed some spiritual powers.

"*I'm here,*" William replied.

"*What's after death?*"

"*I don't know.*"

"*Have you died?*"

"*I think so, but I don't remember.*"

"So it's just empty space?"

"They showed me a large place called Menoram, and it has orange chambers. But I don't remember what it's like there. I'm not sure if we're even conscious when we're there."

"I think I'm going to die in this hospital."

"Your time hasn't arrived yet."

"It's coming. I have a brain tumor."

The door of the hospital room opened, interrupting the silent conversation. Dr. Kamil entered the room, looking brisk and professional. Kenneth's wife sat up, a scowl coming to her face.

"How are you doing, Mr. Daniels? Better?"

Kenneth made a sound as though he were in pain.

Dr. Kamil listened as though the noise made sense. "I see. So, I just wanted to tell you that we're reviewing your case this afternoon, and we may take you off the ventilator if everything checks out. Okay?"

Next to the doctor, his host's wife was steaming mad. "Why the hell did you decide to put him on it in the first place?"

"Well, we may have misread things."

"We?" she said. "It was *you*. You disregarded everybody else's opinion!"

Dr. Kamil held up a hand. "I do apologize if I made a small error in judgment, but in my defense, I wasn't feeling like myself the other day."

She made a huffing sound. "You weren't feeling like *yourself*? What is that supposed to mean?"

"It's hard to explain."

"We're not paying you to not feel like yourself, Dr. Kamil."

He held up his hands. "Please, just give me a bit longer to get the approval. I do need to explain things to my superior."

"We'll be here," said Kenneth's wife.

The doctor nodded curtly, then swiveled on a heel and left the room. William heard him exhale as he left, as though the experience was akin to making a confession.

William's wife looked at him. "Baby, this has been ridiculous. You never should've been here."

An hour later, the respiratory therapist arrived in the room. After some chitchat, William felt her hands on his host's head, and a moment later the plastic tube was being withdrawn from his throat. He felt Kenneth Daniels take a big inhalation . . .

One.

The wife leaned over and kissed him on the cheek.

Snapback.

CHAPTER 27

THE TOP OF THE POD OPENED, AND WILLIAM was up and out of it before Shana could even pull off his cuff.

It felt strange to be in his body again. He was surprised to see most of the team standing around his pod. His eyes scanned their faces. There was Grace, running up and flinging her arms around him. He barely felt it. Then there was Jeremy, throwing an arm across his shoulders. There was Trina, looking significantly better and quietly beaming. Behind them stood Proof. Shana slipped alongside William and quietly took off his cuff.

There was only one person missing.

Hunter.

"Where is he?" William suddenly yelled. "*Where is Hunter?*"

"You're going to have to calm down, William," said Proof.

"I don't *need* to calm down, what I *need* is to get my hands on that piece of . . . "

William felt Grace's arms encircling him, Jeremy's hands on his shoulders, Trina's hands on his back. They were trying to bring him down with love, as expressed through physical touch.

Sure enough, William felt his rage subside, his vision clear. His jaw unclenched. The thick cords on his neck disappeared. He felt his heartbeat return to a rate that was close to normal.

"First, we want to make sure that you're okay," said Grace.

"How long was I gone?" asked William.

"Two days."

Somebody handed him a plastic cup. It was filled with water. William realized that his mouth was dry.

"We couldn't give you any fluids," said Shana, "because we couldn't open the pod while you were still in the tag-along."

"We sat here waiting," said Trina, "almost straight through it all."

"Bro," said Jeremy, "I got so sick of looking at the number four-nine-nine above your pod. Staring at that number for two days. I hate that number now."

William turned. It now read five hundred.

Shana came around to his front and looked into his eyes. She reached forward and lifted his lip, as if she were inspecting a horse. "I think we'd better examine you in the medical bay nonetheless."

"I just spent two straight days in a hospital," said William. "Don't make me spend more time in a medical bay."

"So what happened?" asked Jeremy.

William looked at him, trying to process this. "So Hunter didn't tell you."

"He didn't tell us anything."

William looked at Proof. "You must've found out."

Proof shook his head. "It's a long story."

William felt the story start to flow out of his mouth. "He put me on a ventilator. He was a doctor. I was a patient."

"It was a scenario intended to build trust," said Proof.

"It didn't work. He forced the doctor to put me, er, my host on a ventilator, even when he didn't need it. I was left with one more breath for two days, until the doctor realized his mistake and gave the order to take me off the ventilator."

"Seriously?" said Jeremy.

Trina looked frightened. Grace was listening, but something in her face told William that she wasn't surprised.

"So that's why I want to know where that bastard is," said William. The anger suddenly returned, and he brushed everyone's hands off him. "Where is Hunter?"

Nobody spoke for a moment. Then Grace finally drew a deep breath.

"He's gone," said Grace.

William was taken aback. "What do you mean?"

Proof stepped forward, his basso profundo voice reassuring in a moment of crisis. "What she means is, Hunter has left the team."

CHAPTER 28

A N HOUR LATER, WILLIAM FOUND HIM-
SELF reclining in the medical bay. He'd bathed for
a few minutes, with Shana right outside the door,
periodically knocking to see if he was all right. Then he'd
changed his clothes. Finally, Shana insisted that he rest in the
bay tonight, just in case. He felt healthy, but he decided to
humor her anyway.

Now he had nothing to do but wait for someone to tell
him what happened while he was gone.

To Hunter.

William lay on the mattress, propped up, the sconces on
the walls casting soft indirect light. He watched the light
slowly move through the entire chromatic spectrum every
minute, from red through yellow, green through violet, and
back to red again. It was soothing here, not at all like the horrific experience he'd just escaped from.

The door to the medical bay slid open. He turned his head
and saw Proof enter, wearing a curious expression on his face.

"I was hoping it would be you," said William.

Proof pulled up a seat alongside the bed and looked deep
into William's eyes. "No one's ever gone that long in a snap."

William was partly surprised that he was using the word *snap*. That was the team members' slang. Proof usually used the more formal *tag-along*.

"It felt like a never-ending torture," William said. "A huge plastic tube down my throat, the whole thing taped to my face. My hands were tied to the gurney. Even with sedatives, it's nothing anybody should have to endure."

"Did you notice anything different about this experience? I'm hoping for some insight." Proof was very attentive, his entire body facing William, his ear cocked to the side, as if to hear him better.

William thought about it. "One strange thing was that after I communicated with the host, he started communicating with me."

"Unbidden?"

"Yeah."

He looked mildly surprised. "That means either he has certain abilities, or . . . "

Proof let the thought lapse, but William picked it up. "Or what?"

"Or the longer you stay in a snap, the more you meld with the host."

"Maybe."

They fell silent for a short while, and Proof appeared to be physically uncomfortable.

"So," Proof said. "Don't you want to ask me anything?"

William's eyes flashed with impatience. He had been managing to hold it in. "I was waiting for you to tell me."

"I was waiting for you to ask."

William took the bait. "Okay, okay. Where is Hunter?"

"This is an unbelievable story. I don't know if you're ready for it."

"Try me."

Proof sat back in his chair and crossed his hands on his chest. "Well, first, he comes back from the snap acting like nothing happened."

William felt the anger rising. "Really?"

Proof continued: "After a few minutes, and you don't return, we ask him why you are stuck at four hundred ninety-nine. He says that he doesn't know why. I ask him again if he'd seen you in the snap, since you guys can see each other's nimbus now. He says he never saw you. So then I say, '*Hunter, the purpose of this snap was for the two of you to trust one another. It was designed for you to come in contact with one another. Doctor and patient.*'"

"What did he say?"

"He says that the hospital changed the schedules around and that his host didn't meet your host."

"What a lying bastard."

Proof carried on: "So there you are, stuck at four ninety-nine breaths, and nobody knows what's going on."

"Wait," interrupted William, "I have a question. Can't you personally see what's happening in the snaps?"

"I could, but I choose not to."

William's eyebrows went up. "We always thought you were watching us."

Proof rolled his shoulders. "I'd really prefer to let all of you make your own mistakes. Free will, and all that. So where was I?"

"Nobody knows what's going on," said William.

"Okay, so Hunter disappears into his room. The other team members are flipping out. I'm wondering if I should enter the snap myself to see what's going on with you. I've done that before. And then it happens."

Proof holds his arms out dramatically.

"What?" asked William.

"All the lights went out."

"Where?"

"Here." He made a circle in the air with his finger. "In the corridors, in the rooms, even the power to the pods. It was a total blackout."

William realized that every muscle in his body had tensed up.

"So then a ghostly blue light arrives. It just appears in the middle of the corridor, and it moves down the hall."

"What was it?"

Proof grew animated. "Something ancient! Some unknown entity. But nobody has seen anything like it before."

"Not even you?"

Proof paused and then cocked his head, smiling to himself. "Sometimes I choose to sacrifice some of my abilities. Anyway, we're all gathered in the galley in the dark, watching this thing, this luminous spirit just drifting along. We were totally entranced. Then, it stops in front of Hunter's room."

William felt himself tense up.

"And?"

"We hear Hunter's voice inside the room. He's having an argument with himself, muttering a lot. Then we hear him say,

'No!' Really strange and sharp, almost like a bark. His voice sounded warped."

"Then what?"

Proof took a deep breath. "Well, the blue spirit moves into his room, through the door. I saw it happen. The we hear Hunter scream."

William's jaw dropped open. "This thing was hurting him?"

Proof shrugged. "I don't know. But we hear him shout, 'I don't want it! I don't want it! I don't want it!' That's the truth." He held up one hand like a solemn Boy Scout. "Next thing we know, he comes out of his room, furious, yelling at the top of his lungs in a language that nobody understands."

"Oh my God."

"We see him running, the blue spirit slowly following. He reaches the end of the corridor, where he can't go any farther, and comes back to the galley. The blue spirit still right on him. I'm in the galley with the others, and he comes right up to me and says one word."

"What was it?"

"Menoram."

William thought about that. "He wanted to go back?"

Proof shrugged. "I thought so. I tried to calm him down. I tell him it's going to take some time, and didn't he want to think about this first. Because it's a big decision. It means your spirit will never again be eligible for CA2 or CA3. He says, 'Just start the Blaugrad Mechanism. And hurry.'"

The Blaugrad Mechanism. William whistled low to himself. He remembered hearing something about that during their orientation. It was the way by which a person could voluntarily pull himself or herself off the team. Proof said that nobody had ever tried to use it before.

"Keep in mind," Proof said, "I've never started the Blaugrad Mechanism. It's up to you know who." He pointed at the ceiling, and William guessed that he meant the Ancient Engineer. "So I looked into his eyes to assess his emotional state. Guess what I saw?"

William thought about it. "Fear."

Proof stood up, pointed at William. "You are good. That's exactly what I saw."

William managed a chuckle. "It wasn't hard to guess. He's like two different people. Part of him is afraid of his own antisocial personality."

"Exactly. For a moment, though, I saw the self-aware Hunter, the empathetic one." He paused. "That part of him has been getting smaller and smaller. And I think for a quick second, he knew where this road had been taking him."

"So what finally happened?"

"With everyone standing around, I promise Hunter that I will go and start the Blaugrad Mechanism to return him to Menoram. He runs out of the galley. I stand up and go into the corridor, and I see him backed against the wall by the blue cloud. He's screaming again, almost like a child having a temper tantrum, as the cloud envelops him. And then . . . he . . . "

"He what?"

A look of shock passed across Proof's face. "He just . . . vaporizes. I don't know how to describe it." He paused. "I've handled a lot of teams, but I've never seen an . . . *intrusion* . . . like this."

William couldn't believe his ears. "So you're telling me Hunter just disappeared?"

Proof snapped his fingers. "Just like that. Then the blue cloud just vaporized too. Like it had achieved what it set out to do."

Neither one spoke for a moment. William was fighting a thousand different thoughts and feelings. He swung his legs out of the bed and stood up, alongside Proof. "We need to find out what happened to him. Losing him could throw off the algorithms, and if that happens, then none of us will make CA3."

"I don't think you'll be able to find out where he is," said Proof.

"Why not?"

"This came from high up on the chain."

"Who?"

"Use your imagination. My theory is that someone saw Hunter as a threat, not just to this team, but maybe to the world, or the universe. This was a targeted removal."

"Almost like an execution," William said to himself.

"In a sense, yes." Proof slapped William across the back. "And a day later, you come back. Finally."

"And here we are, at the end of the story."

A mysterious smile came across Proof's face. "No, this is not the end of the story." He stood up, went to the door, and then paused. "Stay here tonight. Stay in the bed. Shana is concerned about possible side effects."

"Okay."

Proof looked at William for a bit longer than necessary,

and then left the medical bay. William lay his head back on the pillow. Tonight he wouldn't be going back to his room, or anywhere.

CHAPTER 29

THAT NIGHT, WILLIAM WAS TORTURED BY thoughts of one person.

Hunter.

He was just one of the five team members, but he'd occupied everybody's thoughts from the first moment they got together. He had huge spirit, not in the *generous* sense, but in the *powerful* sense. After all, Hunter arrived on this team with a dark personality. Then it grew even darker, and on this last snap finally descended into full night. Now he'd been removed from the team by a mysterious blue entity that nobody had seen before.

A term came to William's mind, the perfect term to describe somebody like him.

The Fallen One.

At the very least, Hunter was now spiritually frozen in place. He wouldn't advance to CA3, wouldn't fall to CA0. It wasn't clear what would happen. What did you do with someone who showed so much promise, maybe even more than Grace? Did you abandon him?

They probably wouldn't ever get an answer.

William flipped his pillow over, puffed it, pulled the

blanket over his shoulder. The bay was totally dark now; he'd turned off the colors when he went to bed. He lay there, eyes open in the darkness.

And that's when he saw it.

A figure.

In a chair on the other side of the room sat a shadowy man, his hands placed evenly upon his thighs. His face was indistinct, but he wore a gray wool suit.

William bolted up in his bed. "Who the heck are you?"

The figure turned his head slowly and regarded the human in the bed. William instinctively felt that he wasn't an evil entity, or an icy entity, or a dead entity. But the man was definitely intelligent. William could feel it radiating from his presence.

Then, without warning, William knew who the entity was. He knew as surely as he knew his own name. And when the figure began to speak, William felt a thrill like he'd never known racing through every inch of his body.

"I'm the Ancient Engineer."

The voice was measured, even and thoughtful. It was the voice of every teacher, every boss, every elected official, who had ever commanded respect. It was a deep voice, competent, thorough, compassionate and stern.

William scrambled to catch his breath and his wits. "I'm William." He paused and then added. "Nice to meet you."

He felt incredibly stupid the moment the words escaped his mouth. This was the most powerful spiritual entity in existence, and he'd just introduced himself as though they were cousins at a family reunion.

The Ancient Engineer looked lost in thought for a moment. His mouth opened and closed, as though he were trying to form words. Then he finally spoke.

"You know, there's not many people I can talk to."

William's throat felt scratchy. "Yeah, uh, I bet."

"After all, it's hard to relate to me," he said. "I run the algorithms that govern the universe."

"You're a powerful man."

The Ancient Engineer sighed and rubbed his face. "Don't I know it."

"Don't you want any help? Someone to back you up?"

"I used to, but not anymore."

"What about Proof?"

"He's good with the teams like yours. You know, his specialty is connecting with humans. He likes to focus his energies there."

William didn't know quite what to say next. The Ancient Engineer had appeared in his room and begun an impromptu counseling session. Now he was complaining about his position.

"So what brings you around?" asked William, trying to sound casual.

"Proof did," he said. "He asked me several times for advice about what to do regarding one member of your team. I've been busy, though, so it just got away from me."

"Which member was that?" William knew the answer but asked anyway.

The Ancient Engineer looked at him, his eyes deep and intelligent. "You, William."

William felt his heart skip a beat. That wasn't the answer he was expecting. Suddenly he felt defensive. "That's ludicrous. Nobody looks at me as a problem. In fact, I've been the one trying to . . ."

The Ancient Engineer hushed him by raising a single hand. "That's not why he was talking to me about you."

"Well, then why?"

"You seem to have attracted the attention of a certain spirit. Little Horn."

William thought back to the odd creature in the snap, the one in ancient Persia or wherever, who shook the platform, killed Trina's host, and then climbed up the wall.

"That thing was freaky," he said.

His visitor smiled. "A nice way to put it. That freaky thing is also ancient."

"As ancient as you?"

The engineer smiled. "I'm really not that ancient, William. But Little Horn is an outlier, an entity that has been around since almost the dawn of time. We used to work together, but he chose a different path. Now he has morphed into something almost unrecognizable and very dangerous." He paused. "He's a strange aberration."

"Can he disrupt the system?"

The Ancient Engineer thought about that. "It's fair to say that destruction of humanity is his main focus."

"So what's my role in this?"

The Ancient Engineer stretched his legs. "First, I need something to drink. You want to join me?"

"I'm not supposed to leave this bed," said William.

The Ancient Engineer looked concerned, so William explained. "I was stuck in a tag-along for two days, and they're concerned about the effect on me."

The Ancient Engineer waved a hand over William, emitting a flash of light from his palm.

"You're good now. Meet me in the galley."

The Ancient Engineer literally disappeared. William sat for a minute, stunned, before getting out of the bed.

William walked down the corridor, filled with excitement. It was the middle of the night, and the other team members were asleep in their rooms. He heard Jeremy lightly snoring behind his door.

When William arrived at the galley, the Ancient Engineer was already sitting at the table. A single lamp glowed on the table, illuminating one side of his face, his shoulder, chest and arm. On the table were two glasses of clear liquid.

"You disappeared," said William.

"Sorry," he said, "it's just how I travel. I forget that other people aren't used to it."

"I wish I had shortcuts through time and space," muttered William, taking a seat.

"You will," came the reply. "Proof said that you were highly gifted."

"He's exaggerating."

"No, he's not. I can tell you're sensitive. You'll find them, trust me. After all, I created them." The Ancient Engineer used his thumb and index finger to indicate something small. "They're like these little blips in the framework of your reality. Here's an example. Have you ever been talking to someone and suddenly felt like you've had that exact conversation before, in that exact place, with the same person?"

"Deja vu," said William. "It happens all the time."

He brightened up. "I created that algorithm. Not everybody can access that."

"So, it's a glitch."

"No. It's a feature, not a bug. I add tiny variations on purpose."

"Why?"

"Because predictability is stasis." He paused and then added with a droll intonation, "And stasis is, like, really boring."

"Proof said that you allow evil in the world because it helps us progress."

The Ancient Engineer stretched his arms and looked at the far wall as though he'd just been asked a very difficult question. "No, I actually restrain myself. Good, evil, everything in between, it all serves a purpose. Someday that will change, but not yet." He picked up his glass. "See, it's like a beverage with just the right balance of flavors. I make the ingredient for the liquid. You all have free will to decide the amounts of the ingredients. Then you experience it in the container that I built." He lifted the glass to William. "Cheers."

"Cheers," said William, hoisting his glass. He swallowed the beverage. It really was the perfect balance of sweet, sour, salty, bitter and more.

"Wow," he said. "What is it?"

"I found it in the refrigerator," said the Ancient Engineer, laughing. "You'll have to ask Shana. Proof tells me that she experiments with new beverages when she thinks nobody is looking."

"It's delicious."

They continued drinking in silence. William was positive that this was the strangest encounter he'd ever had, and yet the Ancient Engineer was so personable, so humble, that he felt relaxed. His face was ordinary, unremarkable. His arms were of normal size, his hands too. Overall, he was screamingly average.

The Ancient Engineer noticed William studying him. "I've chosen this shape so that you can relate better to me," he said. "I appeared as a baby walrus to the last team, and one of them tried to stab me."

William felt his jaw fall open. The Ancient Engineer grinned. "That was a joke, William."

"Oh."

"But I have been a baby walrus. It's really weird."

William wasn't expecting this, the designer of the universe to be so playful. And yet it made perfect sense. Whoever created the world had to have a good sense of humor.

"Can we get back to my role with Little Horn?" asked William.

The Ancient Engineer nodded, suddenly somber. "Of course. You're anxious to get on with your mission."

"My mission concerns Little Horn?"

"Well."

"Wait," said William, pushing back from the table. "I didn't even know that I *had* a mission."

"I might've said too much," said the Ancient Engineer. "You don't have a mission, at least not yet. What I *meant* to say was that Little Horn has found you and is tracking you, across tag-alongs. And to advance to CA3, you'll have to deal with him."

A note of panic crept into William's voice. "How do I do that?"

"That's the purpose of my visit." The Ancient Engineer slid a bracelet across the table. It was black, made of a strange polymer, and it was ringed with marks that looked like hieroglyphics. "I would ask you to put this on."

"What is it?"

He waved the question off. "I won't explain now, but it is our ancient Word. Be sure that you wear this before you climb into your pod."

William hesitantly picked up the bracelet and slipped it on his wrist. He immediately felt more attuned to his surroundings. Everything seemed sharper.

"Wow," he said.

"It creates a heightened sense of awareness. Put it on before you get into the pod and you'll have the same sensation in the snap."

"Proof said we have only one tag-along left," muttered William.

"Just one?"

"Yes."

The Ancient Engineer nodded, thinking. "So you're drawing near to the end of the process. Anyway, it'll help. You'll need it against Little Horn."

William blanched. "Do I have to fight him?"

The Ancient Engineer shook his head no. "For the simple reason that no man can defeat him, but you can resist him. This will help you do that when he comes after you."

"Thank you," said William, slipping off the bracelet. The world got a little duller. "Can I ask about Hunter?"

A brief spasm of pain flashed across the Ancient Engineer's face. "What would you like to know?"

"Is he off the team?"

"Yes."

"Where did he go?"

"I can't reveal that."

"What was the blue thing that they said came in here?"

The Ancient Engineer grinned. "That was a special thing I was playing around with a while ago. It was kind of a mistake, but I use it now and then for retrieval."

"So will we see him again?"

"No, he's gone."

"He tried to kill me in the snap."

The Ancient Engineer sighed. "Sometimes there are individuals who are gifted, but who lack the spiritual intuition to find good."

"Is he one of those people?"

He seemed loath to say anything else, so William let it drop. Then the Ancient Engineer yawned. "Time doesn't mean much to me, but still, it's time for me to go."

Scrambling for words, William said, "Well, thanks for dropping by."

The Ancient Engineer nodded and then disappeared. A

second later, William was alone in the galley, a bracelet in his hand and a sense that whatever was coming next, it wasn't going to be easy.

CHAPTER 30

THE LAST DAY.

The four remaining members of the team; William, Grace, Jeremy and Trina sat at the breakfast table in the galley, slowly chewing. It was the morning of their final snap, and while it should've been a happy day, it wasn't.

Hunter wasn't the most popular member of the team. He wore everybody down with his insistent selfishness, his personality always balanced on the knife's edge. But the hard fact remained that he'd been a part of the team, and his descent into betrayal and deceit had cast a dark cloud over what should've been a joyful moment.

"I feel like this should have been more exciting," said Jeremy, morosely pushing food across his plate with a fork.

Grace sighed. "Hunter screwed us up. We can't advance unless all of us advance."

"Maybe we're still advancing," said William. "This is an exceptional situation."

"Maybe," Trina said, "but Proof doesn't know. And they're not telling us anything."

William stayed conspicuously silent, and the other three waited for his input. Trina's eyes landed on his wrist. "What is that?"

He looked down. She was pointing at the bracelet that the Ancient Engineer had given him.

"It's a bracelet," he replied.

"Well, duh," said Trina. "Who gave it to you?"

William swallowed hard and decided that it would be better to lie. "Shana. It's supposed to calm anxiety, and she said I would feel better if I wore it during our final snap."

"That was nice of her," said Grace. "Do you feel anxiety now?"

William took a deep breath and then released it. He felt his chest quiver a little, his hands tremble. "Honestly, yes. I do."

Trina peered at the etchings on the bracelet. "What do those mean?"

William told the truth. "I have no idea." He set down his fork. "Are we all ready to advance to CA3?"

"I don't think it's going to happen," said Jeremy.

"All we can do is try," replied William, standing up from the table.

A few minutes later, the four members of the team stood in the door of the pod tank, looking at the casket-like shapes. William was having trouble processing the idea that this would be the final time he went into a snap. The team had done nearly fifty of them by this point, and he'd started to enjoy sliding into other people's bodies for a few minutes.

"Come on in, don't be shy," said Shana. She was standing in the corner, waiting. "They're the same pods."

Overhead, the parallax was softly playing. "So who wants to choose the last one?"

"I nominate William," said Jeremy, "just to calm his anxiety."

"Any objections?" asked Grace. Nobody voiced any, so she nodded at him. "It's all yours. What are you thinking?"

William tapped his front tooth with an index finger. "Someplace modern and *no more hospitals.*"

They laughed at that, which broke some of the tension and allowed the other three members to relax a little. One by one, they climbed into their pods.

"Hey guys," said Jeremy, "in all seriousness, I really *don't* want to go back to Menoram. So let's do this right."

For a moment, the four teammates looked at each other, and then they lay down in the pods. Shana affixed the cuffs and closed the tops.

William looked up at the parallax. He saw symbolic eagles and large rallies. It looked like a scene from the twentieth century. That would be safe. Nobody would force him onto a ventilator there.

He chose it.

CHAPTER 31

S *NAP.*

In the blink of an eye, William found himself standing in a line of people wearing what looked like gray sacks. They were trudging forward, their shoulders slumped, feet shuffling ahead. All of them had been shaved bald.

Five hundred breaths.

He looked down at his hands. They were small and delicate. He looked at his feet. They were miniscule. Then he realized what had happened.

He'd snapped into a child.

A little girl, from the looks of it. She was really cold. Her chest was shivering and her feet felt like lumps of frozen clay. William's heart instantly went out to the poor girl. He could feel the deep sadness and fear within her.

Next to him, another line of people trudged along. A woman turned her head toward him. Her eyes were hollow and dead in their sockets. "Katarina," she said, "you must tell them your name."

Four hundred sixty-two. Four hundred sixty-one.

William waited in line, head bowed. And then he looked ahead. At a small wooden table were a doctor, a nurse and a military officer. The officer carried a pistol in a holster at his waist. His jacket was emblazoned with an insignia showing an eagle holding a cross that was bent at all four corners.

William knew that insignia. It was a swastika.

He was in a concentration camp in Nazi Germany. He felt a flash of incredible regret and pain. He'd accidentally chosen to experience one of the worst moments of human history.

The line inched forward. As they drew closer to the table, William could see that the doctor was opening each person's mouth and inspecting their teeth. He could see the doctor lifting the people's arms to gauge muscle tone. If sufficient health was determined, the doctor jerked a thumb toward the nurse, on the right. She was leading the people into a large warehouse.

For the others, the people who presumably failed the health test, the doctor gestured to the officer, on the left. He was guiding people to a ramp and loading them onto a waiting train, like cattle.

He glimpsed a yellow nimbus ahead in line. That was Trina. A blue nimbus was behind him. That was Jeremy. An orange nimbus was being escorted by the nurse into the warehouse. Grace.

Three hundred seventy-four. Three hundred seventy-three.

His host inched forward in line, shivering. He felt her scrunch her tiny toes in a futile effort to stay warm. Futile, because the air was nearly freezing. The party officials were wearing thick pea coats and leather gloves.

The man in front of him was given the thumb to the left, and William watched his entire body sag. He wouldn't move, so the officer came and propelled him roughly by the arm toward the ramp and the cattle train.

Then the officer looked down at William's host. He had short blonde hair, clear blue eyes, and a strong jaw. His face was cruel in its indifference. Then William saw it.

Coming into focus around the man's head was a black nimbus.

"Hunter," he said.

"William."

"Shouldn't you be in Menoram?" William asked. *"How did you get here without the pod?"*

"I can do anything I want. I've grown more powerful than you could ever believe."

Hunter delivered that last line like he meant it, and William didn't have reason to doubt. To occupy someone's body without a pod was impossible unless you surrendered to a different power, an evil power.

William's attention jerked back to the tag-along. His tiny host had stepped to the front of the line. She was facing the nurse and the doctor.

"Name," said the nurse.

The little girl said nothing.

"Name!" shouted the nurse, her brow creasing in anger.

"You have to tell them your name," said William.

She must've heard him, because the girl finally squeaked out an answer. "Katarina."

"Last name?" said the nurse.

She wouldn't speak. She turned her head and looked at the hollow-eyed woman in the next line. The woman's lower lip was trembling, but she said nothing.

William decided to help the girl again. *"If you don't tell them your last name, you will never see your mother again."*

He'd guessed it was her mother, and he was right. Katarina turned back to the nurse. "Katarina Berghoff."

The doctor crouched down. His eyes were clinical blue, as cold as an iceberg. "Open your mouth, Katarina Berghoff."

William felt his host's tiny mouth open. The doctor inserted a gloved finger into the aperture. He was close enough to see the doctor's eyelashes, his fuzzy eyebrows, his flared nostrils, the tiny bits of hair at the edge of his beard. He felt the doctor's finger probing the teeth.

Then the doctor removed his finger and wiped it on a towel. "I want you to jump, Katarina Berghoff."

"Where?"

"Up into the air. Here, touch my hand."

The doctor held his hand about half a meter above William's head.

William's host turned back toward her mother. "Jump for him, Katarina."

"Jump," said William. *"Your life depends on it."*

He felt his tiny body compress itself into a crouch and then explode upward in a large leap. Her hand missed the doctor's by a few centimeters.

"Almost," said the doctor, studying the child's body. "Do it again."

Katarina crouched down and leapt up again. This time her fingertips grazed the doctor's palm. William felt his host's little body fall onto the ground.

"Very good," said the doctor, nodding to the nurse. "Pick

yourself up and follow the nurse. We have something special planned for you."

William's host pulled herself to her feet and toddled toward the nurse, who gestured for her to follow.

"Katarina!" a voice shouted.

It was the girl's mother. William felt his host break into a panic, and she bolted back and wrapped her arms around her mother's legs.

Two hundred twenty-two. Two hundred twenty-one.

Hunter was on him in an instant. William felt the officer's strong hands on his little shoulders, and he was hauled off the woman's legs. He felt the mother grabbing him and pulling him back.

"Don't take her!" shouted the mother.

"Stand down!" shouted the officer.

"It's my baby! She stays with me!"

The officer pulled his weapon from his holster and pointed it at the woman's head. "She comes with us."

The host's mother clenched her jaw tightly. Her lips became a thin bloodless white line in her gray face. She bent down and slowly unpeeled the girl's tiny fingers from around her leg.

"Go with the man," she said.

"No," William heard Katarina's voice say.

"Go. You must."

The officer finally yanked William away. Hunter's host's strong hand found the space between William's tiny shoulder blades and pushed him. William stumbled a few steps and fell onto the dirt.

The officer started back to his position next to the table,

but after a couple of steps, he stopped, as though he'd forgotten something. His face changed its expression. A dark, horrific look spread across his face like rancid butter.

He turned back. He lifted his pistol and shot the woman in the side of the head.

The mother's blood splattered across the person behind her, and the woman's body crumpled to the frozen dirt. The other gray figures standing in line were shocked, but nobody dared react.

William cried out and then felt a strong hand clamp across the mouth.

One hundred forty-nine. One hundred forty-eight.

He found himself being carried in the arms of the nurse into the warehouse and placed in a small holding pen with a group of other people. Three guards with rifles at the ready stood on an observation platform, looking down on them.

The little girl sat down on the floor and cradled her knees in her arms. William felt incredibly sorry for his host. He'd never known the internal anguish felt by a small child who watched her mother be killed. This was another level of empathy, understanding the absolute worst thing that could happen to a person. He couldn't imagine anything that would rip apart a young soul worse than this.

The little girl looked up. Through her eyes, William watched the people milling around. Some were hunchbacked and elderly. One was mentally handicapped. Others were healthy. William wondered what exactly was the criteria for entering this warehouse. Then he decided that he didn't want to know.

Seventy-two. Seventy-one.

A minute later, he felt the hair stand up on his arms. There was a presence nearby, one that he'd felt before. Something strange and ancient.

Scanning the room, he saw it. It was humanoid, with four limbs and a face, and it was creeping along the observation platform behind the guards. Its pale white skin was carpeted with a creepy blanket of small horns.

It was Little Horn.

William's blood instantly ran cold. Somehow this time the fear was even greater, because the Ancient Engineer had described the entity in more detail.

"Don't move," he told the little girl.

Katarina sat stock still, her thin arms locked around her knees. He watched Little Horn creep along the platform and then descend slowly down one of the pillars until it landed on the dirt. It stood up to its full height, which seemed nearly eight feet tall, and scanned the sad gray people penned in the concentration camp warehouse.

Then the creature spotted him. It move through the sad gray people. They paid no attention to it.

"They can't see it," William said. *"Only we can. Now close your eyes, quickly."*

She obeyed. William could feel Little Horn drawing closer. He was suddenly glad for the bracelet that the Ancient Engineer had given him.

The little girl's skin went cold. It was as though ice water had been tapped directly into the space between her eyes.

Forty-three. Forty-two.

She opened her eyes. Little Horn's face was right in front of hers, its enormous humanoid body crouched down before this tiny, pathetic girl shivering on the cold ground. The creature was so close that William could feel every icy breath. He saw the tiny horns on the creature's skin pulsing, opening and closing, like horrific little carnivorous flowers.

"*William,*" said Little Horn.

William didn't reply.

"*You can't run from me forever,*" the creature said.

The little girl was trembling. Little Horn lifted a hand, as though it were going to snatch the girl's eyes out of her skull.

Than Little Horn stopped. Its face turned slightly. It rose to its feet and moved away.

Katarina turned around to watch it. Behind her, another person had entered the pen, a sad gray man with a blue nimbus around his head.

Jeremy.

Leaving the little girl behind, Little Horn made a beeline for him and immediately pounced. Jeremy's host fell to the ground, writhing beneath the power of the ancient horror.

"*William!*" shouted Jeremy. "*Help me!*"

"*What do you want me to do?*"

"*I don't know! Do something!*"

Jeremy's host lay on the ground, struggling under his invisible enemy. William could only imagine how strange this looked to the other people in the warehouse pen. He briefly wondered about people in other times and other settings who appeared to be possessed. How many of them were struggling with invisible demonic entities?

Little Horn was sprawled across the man, as though it were in a wrestling match. William realized that it was moving its skin across the skin of Jeremy's host. He could hear dozens of small smacking sounds. It was the sound of something feeding.

"*Oh God,*" said Jeremy, "*please stop him. He's taking me. He's too powerful.*"

Katarina leapt to her feet and ran across the floor of the pen.

William tried to stop her. "*No, Katarina!*"

The little girl pounced on the demon's arm. With the flick of it wrist, Little Horn flung her through the air. She sailed clear across the warehouse and landed on a pile of sacks.

Ten. Nine.

William felt the girl's pain. "*You can't fight it, Katarina. You have to avoid it instead.*"

She looked at Little Horn. It had finished with Jeremy's host and stood up. The body of the man was slick with blood, twitching like a dying frog.

"*Jeremy?*" said William. "*Are you okay?*"

At first, there was no response. Then Jeremy's host stood up. The blue nimbus was gone. His eyes landed on William's. They looked different.

"*It's your turn, William.*"

That wasn't Jeremy's voice. It was Little Horn's. Jeremy's host bounded across the floor with an unearthly power and speed.

One.

Katarina took in a sharp breath.

Snapback.

CHAPTER 32

WILLIAM WOKE UP IN THE POD AND immediately pounded on the cover with the heels of his hands. Through the glass he saw Shana arrive. A few seconds later, the lid slid open. She undid his cuff and he leapt out.

Violent scratching came from Jeremy's pod. It sounded like a wild animal was trapped inside. Shana's brow creased, and she went over to open it.

"Don't!" shouted William. "Don't touch it!"

She looked at him, confused. "What do you mean? It's just Jeremy, and he wants to get out!"

William ran over to Jeremy's pod and threw himself between Shana and the release button. "Something happened, and I think we need to talk to Proof before we let Jeremy out."

She looked skeptical, and his eyes pleaded with hers.

"All right," she said.

"I'll release Trina and Grace," he said, "while you find Proof."

She disappeared into the corridor, and William opened Trina and Grace's pods. The two women sat up and wiped the conducting foam from their shoulders.

"William, what happened?" asked Grace.

"I heard you and Jeremy talking, and then there was just . . . nothing," added Trina.

He just pointed to Jeremy's pod. Inside, Jeremy was snorting and snarling and scratching like a wild beast.

"What happened?"

"We ran into Little Horn."

"Oh."

"And it kind of . . . *ate* Jeremy's host."

Trina's mouth opened. "You mean like a cannibal?"

"No," said William. "It's kind of hard to describe. It ate the host with its skin."

Grace covered her mouth with her hand. "Oh my God."

Trina looked like she was going to be sick.

"And that's the result," he said, jerking his thumb at the pod.

Proof entered the room. He glanced at Jeremy's pod, heard the grunts and scrapes. A look of concern appeared on his face. "William, tell me what happened. Quickly now."

William repeated the story, and when finished, Proof looked stricken, but in control. He went over to Jeremy's pod and looked down at the snarling creature within. Then he looked up at the other team members.

"This doesn't have to be your concern," he said.

"Why not?" asked William.

Proof's eyes lighted on each of the three remaining team members. "Because you're going to CA3."

A smile spread across Trina's face in spite of the present situation. "Really?"

He nodded. "I've coached a lot of teams, and all the signs are there. Everything is lined up."

"So you're saying that Jeremy doesn't matter?" asked Grace.

Proof shrugged. "It's our problem, not yours. You don't need to think about this." His hand thumped lightly on the pod.

William, Grace and Trina looked at each other as if searching for answers. "But I thought you said that we all have to advance as a unit," said William. "First we lost Hunter."

"The Ancient Engineer made an exception for that," said Proof.

"And now we lose Jeremy."

"You had it before this," said Proof. "You've advanced to CA3. The only question is . . . "

"Do we want this weighing on our consciences," finished William. He sighed and began pacing the room, his hands thrust deep into his pockets. "That's really it, isn't it? The reason for this entire parallax exercise was to learn empathy. Would it make any sense for us to abandon it now?"

"But what can we do?" asked Grace. "We essentially have Little Horn trapped inside this pod."

"I don't know," said William.

He thought about it. "We could go back for another snap, if Proof would let us. And maybe we could defeat Little Horn there."

Trina butted in. "What good would *that* do? It's Little Horn. You said that nobody knows how to fight it."

"If we could find it, instead of the other way around," said William, "then maybe I could catch it by surprise."

"And then what?" said Grace. "You could frighten Little Horn? Say boo?"

"There's another risk," said Proof. "Right now your CA3 status is assured. But you could lose that status if you mess this up."

"How?"

"Do something violent. Attack somebody. Anything that requires loss of empathy. So you'd better figure out how you're going to do that."

The scraping from Jeremy's pod grew stronger. Then he started punching the sides of the pod. They could see stress fractures forming.

"Whatever you decide," said Shana, "it should be done pretty fast."

The three team members looked at each other. "Should we do it?" asked William.

"We're following you," said Trina. Her eyes glanced at his bracelet. "You've got the magic thing."

"William, I was meaning to ask you, what is that?" asked Shana.

Trina looked at William. He felt acutely embarrassed. "You don't remember giving that to me?"

"I never gave that to you," she said.

Now all eyes were on William.

"Stop lying and tell us where you got that," said Grace.

William took a deep breath and decided to come clean. "The Ancient Engineer gave it to me."

Grace was aghast. Shana's jaw nearly hit the floor. Even Proof sat back and looked at William with new eyes.

"You met him?" asked Trina.

"Yep." William tried to make it sound like no big deal.

"What's he like?" asked Grace.

"Pretty normal, really. But he gave me this bracelet and said it would protect me against Little Horn."

Grace grabbed his wrist and studied it. "What are those etchings?"

"I really don't know," he replied.

"Let me see it," said Proof.

William removed the bracelet and handed it to the team coach. Proof studied the etchings, peering closely.

"This is a script I haven't seen for a long time," he said.

"Where does it come from?" asked Grace.

Proof shook his head. "It would take too long to explain. But I think I can understand what it says."

They all waited expectantly. At last Proof looked up. "Oh, do you want me to tell you?"

"Yes!!" the team all shouted. Even Shana had positioned herself alongside them.

"It says that Little Horn has a weakness."

"What is it?" they asked in unison.

"*Water*. It hates living water."

William nodded. It made sense, since water was the single element that gave life. Little Horn, on the other hand, sought to *take away* life.

A huge crack sounded from Jeremy's pod. The top was nearly broken.

"We have to decide now," said Grace.

"Let's do it," said William.

"There's no coming back if Little Horn gets you," said Proof.

"It won't," William replied, climbing into the pod. Then he looked up at the others. "Aren't you coming?"

Trina and Grace climbed into their pods. Shana affixed the armbands to each one, the sound of shouts and barks and punches sounding ever louder from Jeremy's pod.

"Is he going to snap with us?" said Trina, motioning toward Jeremy's pod.

"He'd better," said Proof. "Otherwise, we have a bigger problem on our hands." He clapped William on the shoulder. "Godspeed."

"You know I'm going to have to take full control of my host," said William.

"I do know," said Proof, "but you didn't tell me that."

Proof tried to hand the bracelet from the Ancient Engineer back to William, but he refused it. "No. It's time for me to have faith. I'm supposed to be the bait."

Shana affixed the cuff to his arm. "You be careful, William."

He smiled. "You're a good egg, Shana. You know we couldn't have done any of this without you."

"Good luck, William," she said. Then she slid the pod shut.

The parallax appeared overhead. They hadn't assigned the selection to anyone, but William assumed it was up to him to decide.

He saw an image of an ocean, a body of water, and chose it.

CHAPTER 33

S *NAP.*

William found himself aboard an aircraft carrier, wearing a sailor's white long-sleeve shirt, neckerchief, and round white cap. His pants were bright white and his shoes gleaming black. He figured out right away that he was in the navy.

Five hundred breaths.

It was a long cruiser, with a pair of anti-aircraft cannons, one fore and one aft. He was chatting with another sailor, who looked to be all of nineteen years old. A plug of tobacco bulged out of the sailor's cheek. He was gesturing to something on his foot when an alarm sounded.

Awooooooooga! Awooooooooga!

It was the klaxon. Incoming!

William's host and the other sailor instantly broke into a run. They fled across the deck and then scampered up a ladder to the front of the ship.

Four hundred sixty-four. Four hundred sixty-three.

William felt himself hyperventilating. The stress of the incoming attack had pulled his fight-or-flight trigger, and the adrenaline was elevating all of his bodily systems: blood pressure, cortisol, respiration. He knew he would have much less time than usual in this snap.

Which meant that he had to find Little Horn quickly. He decided to call to it telepathically.

"I'm here," William said.

While his host battened down hatches and readied life-boats, William waited for a response. There was none, so he shouted again.

"Little Horn! I'm here!"

His host stopped moving and looked around. William knew that he'd heard the telepathic shout, which meant that he had a few abilities. William decided to speak to his host directly.

"You're about to be attacked," he said, *"and you'll need to let me guide you."*

"Who is this?"

William ignored the question. *"It won't be an enemy you can see. It will be an ancient entity. It's called Little Horn."*

He could feel that his host was thoroughly confused. *"Who is this?"*

William ignored the question again. *"When it comes, I'm going to take over your body. You're going to find yourself doing some strange things. Is that okay?"*

Pause. Then the sailor asked, *"Do I have a choice?"*

"No."

"Okay."

William tried to shout one more time. *"Little Horn you unholy freak, you wanted a fight and I'm going to give it to you! Come find me!"*

The klaxon was still blaring. *Awooooooooga! Awooooooooga!* William found himself climbing down a ladder, through a hatch, into the bowels of the ship. The corridors were so narrow that men had to turn sideways to pass one another. Everything was illuminated a sickly red from the fluorescent lights behind steel cages.

His host ran down the corridor and then dashed right. He ducked his head and passed through a low doorway and entered what seemed to be the infernal bowels of hell.

It was the engine room.

Three hundred thirty-seven. Three hundred thirty-six.

On either side of him the engines towered three stories high. The room stank of oil and iron and fire. The sailors who worked here, the grease monkeys, were strange-looking creatures. They held wrenches and hung from rafters and clung to catwalks.

As William moved through the room, he noted that fear had settled upon their faces.

"William," said a voice.

He froze. He knew that voice. It was Jeremy's. William looked around and quickly spotted the host.

A young sailor was perched on a catwalk overhead, a light blue nimbus encircling his head. But William forced himself to remember that Little Horn had swallowed Jeremy's soul. That wasn't Jeremy up there, and it wasn't Jeremy's host either.

It was Little Horn.

William summoned all his energy and yelled at Little Horn at the top of his telepathic lungs. *"Leave Jeremy! Leave the host! I want to see you alone!"*

"Try to make me," said Jeremy's voice.

Suddenly the host leapt onto a large, slowly turning vertical gear. With superhuman agility, he slid down the side, hit the ground, and crept toward William. As the young sailor drew closer, William could see that he was covered in grease, smudged head to toe in black gunk. The only thing visible in the dark maw of his face were the whites of his eyes.

And they looked positively demonic.

Two hundred seventy-two. Two hundred seventy-one.

William took over his own host now. In the blink of an eye, he fully inhabited the young man's mind, the spirit, the body. It came so easily, he was surprised that he'd had difficulty doing so in past snaps.

"Jeremy isn't the one you want," said William. *"I'm the one you want."*

The sailor drew close to him, so close that they were nose to nose.

"Humans have need for power."

"Some of us already have it," said William. *"I'm CA3."*

The sailor laughed. It began like a human sound and then slowly transformed into a horrendous alien cackle. The sailor stepped back, clutched his head, and collapsed on the grate.

William stood looking at him, until he became aware of a presence at his side.

It was Little Horn, in its regular guise: humanoid shape, pale white skin, flat face with no features.

"You."

William took off running, back through the low gate to

the engine room. He looked back over his shoulder. Little Horn was just a few paces behind, cackling gleefully.

"Run Change Agent, he might get you!"

Little Horn could taunt him all he wanted, but William knew that his task had been achieved. It'd taken a lot of taunting, but Jeremy was free of Little Horn.

He dashed down the ghastly red corridor, which was blissfully free of other sailors.

Awooooooooga! Awooooooooga!

The klaxon was still going, stronger and stronger. He could hear the sound of airplanes droning overhead, growing louder.

"You're going to die," said Little Horn.

William had neither the breath nor the force to answer. He had one destination in mind.

The ocean.

One hundred fifty-six. One hundred fifty-five.

Still running, William arrived at the ladder that led up to the hatch on the ship's deck. He threw himself onto the ladder, grabbed hold, and scampered up the rungs. Halfway up, something grabbed his ankle. He looked back.

Little Horn had caught up. Its smooth white face was distorted into a caricature of hate. Its eyebrows angled downward, its eyes squinted into thin sharp slits, and it was showing its black teeth.

"Change Agent, Change Agent, where do you think you're going?"

William tried to shake its hand off, but the grip was unreal. Little Horn had a strength far beyond its shape.

"Let me go and we'll fight this on the deck," said William.

The ancient entity made a horrible gurgling response. It opened its jaws and fastened its mouth around the sailor's ankle. William screamed in pain. It felt like red-hot knitting needles being jammed into his host's body.

Ninety-eight. Ninety-seven.

William was halfway turned around on the ladder now, his arm hooked around it. He kicked harshly, but Little Horn wouldn't release him. The ancient creature made small barks and growls like an animal that had just discovered a new favorite toy.

Then William saw something that made his blood run cold.

The small horns on the creature's skin began to open and close as if yearning to devour human flesh and human spirit, and this time, he was going to be the victim.

"Get off!" William shouted.

"You're mine," said Little Horn.

Panicking, William hauled his arm back to sock the creature, but before he could, an enormous explosion shook the ship. It was a deafening noise that shook William to his teeth. Immediately came the sound of steel rending, and then the ladder lurched to the side.

Hanging on as the ladder pitched over, William felt the rung tight underneath his armpit. Little Horn had been caught unaware. The pale humanoid released William's ankle and flailed for a grip. Too late. It tumbled down the ladder and hit the bottom.

William didn't waste a minute watching it. His overriding goal was to lure it up to the deck.

Fifty-two. Fifty-one.

William pulled himself up the remaining rungs to the hatch. It had already been closed in preparation for the attack, so he quickly turned the crank. Seven, eight, nine revolutions before a sliver of daylight shined through the rims of the hatch.

Forty-three. Forty-two.

A moment later, he pushed the hatch open and climbed out into the daylight. The smell of exploded munitions assaulted his nostrils. The deck was a wreck, a missile or bomb had ripped open an enormous hole on the starboard side of the ship. It was a tangle of twisted metal and smoking debris. A few bloody corpses lay on the deck, the casualties of war.

William moved across the deck, barely noticing the other sailors, the wounded ones, crying out for help. People had lived, fought and died throughout history. His actions here would save perhaps one, but he had a bigger goal to remember.

Twenty-five. Twenty-four.

He looked back at the hatch. It was open, empty, waiting for the ancient entity to climb up through it and give chase.

"Where are you?" he said to Little Horn.

At that moment, the humanoid burst from the hatch like a person shot out of a cannon. It leapt fifteen meters into the air and landed on the deck.

"Prepare to be lost," it hissed.

Little Horn loped toward William. Its strange splayed feet slapped against the deck, and its little slitted eyes were zeroed in on its prey.

Twelve. Eleven.

Even though William had prepared for this moment in his mind, he wasn't ready to experience it. An outlier, a strange aberration. That's what the Ancient Engineer had called Little Horn. He also had called him dangerous.

"My friend," said a familiar voice.

William twisted around. Another sailor stood behind him, feet splayed wide apart, a demonic grin plastered across his face. A black nimbus floated like an evil mist around his head.

It was Hunter.

"I'm not your friend," said William.

"I wasn't talking to you," Hunter hissed.

William rolled to the side just as Little Horn leapt, and the ancient evil entity ran smack into Hunter's host. He tackled the man to the ground and began to devour him, the same way he'd done to Jeremy's host, but this time there was no resistance. Hunter was welcoming it.

Horrified, William scooted backward, away from the tiny horned plants opening and closing on the entity's skin. Hunter's host had a terrific smile plastered on his face as a slick of fresh blood spread on the deck beneath him.

Satisfied and soaked in the sailor's blood, Little Horn stood up. A black nimbus was wreathed around it head. *"That feels better,"* it said.

William cocked his head. He wasn't sure if he'd heard Little Horn's voice or Hunter's voice. They seemed to have melded together.

"But I need more, William. I need you."

The ancient entity advanced toward him once more.

William took a step backward, and then another step, but Little Horn accelerated suddenly. In the blink of an eye, the creature was upon him, and William found himself tackled flat on his back, Little Horn on top of him.

"You're mine!"

"Never!" said William.

Little Horn gripped his wrists. William felt the tiny carnivorous flowered horns of his skin opening and closing. They were starting to absorb his host's body. It was bizarre and disgusting. Even worse, he could feel himself weakening, his life force draining.

Nine. Eight.

Another massive explosion ripped through the port side of the ship. This time, William felt the shock wave, the blast of heat, much more intensely than he had on the ladder. He felt his body, and Little Horn, lifted by the force and carried several meters to the right.

When he landed, William felt a searing pain on his right side. He looked down. Hot bits of metal shrapnel were burning into his body. In fact, his whole right side was peppered with small holes.

A short distance away, Little Horn woke up and began to slowly crawl toward him.

"You're mine!" the creature said.

"Can't you say anything else?" replied William

"Die!"

That voice sounded more like Hunter's. The figure leapt into the air with almost unnatural strength. William glanced to his left. He was less than a meter from the edge of the deck.

Below that, and spread out to the horizon, was the blue carpet of the ocean.

As Little Horn was about to fall upon him, William rolled toward the edge.

Six. Five.

He scrambled to his feet, the back of his black sailor's boots at the edge of the ship.

"Come and get me," said William.

Little Horn looked at him, the slitted eyes looking reptilian.

Three.

It sprang at William, who ripped the neckerchief from his neck and wrapped it around Little Horn's. The creature screamed and then sank its blackened teeth into William's forearm.

The pain was so intense that William teetered in his shoes, began to fall backward, grabbed the neckerchief, and pulled Little Horn over the edge of the ship with him.

Two.

Together, the two hurtled eighty feet down, along the hull, through the air. As the ocean rushed up to meet them, William held his breath in anticipation.

His last breath.

One.

They hit the water, plunging deep before their momentum slowed.

His lungs full of air, William waited for his body to rise back to the surface. He didn't dare breathe out yet, even though it would've ended the snap, because he didn't want this host to find himself fifteen feet underwater. He needed to at least get the man's body to the surface. His full lungs would also help him rise to the surface more quickly.

He saw Little Horn floating next to him, in a fetal position, eyes closed, the picture of helplessness. "He's weaker in water," Proof had said. William knew he could put faith in Proof's words.

He paused. This was William's chance to kill this horrific entity, this bizarre evil blip in the world, once and for all. This was the opportunity to do the universe a favor.

He had to do it.

Looking around, William saw a piece of twisted metal drop into the water and begin sinking. It had evidently just fallen off the carrier. He kicked his way over to the metal and caught it just before it passed into the dark abyss beneath his feet. William looked at the debris in his hand. It was a piece of aluminum steel panel, twisted and ripped and still hot to the touch.

Holding onto it tightly, and still holding onto his final breath, William swam back to Little Horn. Without wasting a second, he pulled his arm back to run the twisted metal into the entity. But before he could strike, the creature spun around and caught his arm. Little Horn was undoubtedly slower in water, but it was still powerful.

"*You're mine*," Little Horn hissed.

"*Saying it won't make it true,*" said William.

They grappled over the metal, the two of them suspended a few meters below the surface. William pushed; Little Horn blocked. It was strange fighting underwater. It felt like performing jujitsu in a tank of syrup.

Without oxygen, though, William felt his strength starting to leave him. Before he knew it, Little Horn was slowly forcing the pointed end of the twisted metal toward his body. Then Little Horn's hand found William's throat and squeezed. William felt his limbs go soft. This was going horribly wrong. He couldn't die here. Snapping into a host who died would be grounds for him to lose his CA3 status.

"*You can't kill me,*" said Little Horn. "*Nobody has ever killed me.*"

"*Watch me,*" William gasped.

"*I'll come back. I always do.*"

"*The Ancient Engineer said you're nothing but a mistake in the universe,*" replied William. "*Your entire existence is a strange aberration. We humans are the flower of creation. That's why you have spent your entire existence trying to destroy us.*"

"*There's something he isn't telling you,*" said Little Horn.

"*What is it?*"

"*I was a Change Agent Level Three.*"

"*Liar!*"

"*There's a lot the Ancient Engineer doesn't want to tell you,*" he hissed.

There was no way to tell if the creature was lying or telling the truth, but it didn't matter. This was intolerable news. But William knew in his heart what was true. The Ancient Engineer loved them and wanted them to succeed. That thought sent a bolt of courage through William's mind and body. Howling out in anguish, he grabbed a hold of the piece of metal, turned it back on Little Horn, and ran it through the ancient entity's abdomen. Instantly, the creature's grip on his throat loosened. An unearthly howl emitted from its mouth. Large bubbles rose slowly to the surface, while dark blood pumped into the water, forming a poisonous cloud that looked like squid ink.

A single tendril of the cloud brushed William's skin. It burned like acid, and he jerked backward. Quickly, he kicked away from the bleeding entity, his lungs nearly bursting. Without wasting a second, he pushed himself up to the surface with three powerful kicks.

"Goodbye, Little Horn. Goodbye, Hunter."

A moment later, William breached the surface and gasped as he released his final breath. He started to suck in another enormous lungful of air.

Snapback.

CHAPTER 34

WILLIAM AWOKE IN HIS POD. HE STILL had the sensation of being trapped underwater, unable to breathe, and so he spent a minute just lying still, breathing.

Then he opened his eyes. There was no movement outside the pod. "Shana?" he called.

There was no response, so he pounded on the cover of the pod with the heels of his palms. "Shana? Proof?"

Still nothing. The only sound was the occasional beep of the monitor that Shana kept in the corner of the room. William screamed her name as loudly and for as long as he could. He kicked the pod cover with his feet. He threw a temper tantrum like a child.

At last he ran out of breath and lay there, gasping. The sad truth was starting to occur to him: Nobody was coming for him. Shana had abandoned the team, and apparently Proof had too. Maybe they figured that he'd be killed by Little Horn. Maybe they'd been reassigned to a different task. Maybe the Change Agent program had been discontinued by the Ancient Engineer.

Or maybe something else had happened, something he hadn't foreseen.

No matter what, it was up to him to get himself out.

William recalled that the polymer lids of the pods were pretty much unbreakable, at least without power tools. However, the corner joints of the pod casket could be gamed. They were riveted, as he remembered.

So kicked at the right corner of the pod, over and over. He could feel it giving way, just a little. His right leg tired, so he flipped over onto his belly and continued bashing the corner with his left leg.

At last, the bottom piece of the pod loosened from the base. Two more good kicks, and it swung free completely. William undid the armband and scooted himself down the pod and slipped out the narrow aperture at the end, falling onto the floor of the pod tank.

He lay there for a moment, breathing heavily, before pulling himself to his feet. He looked around. Everything appeared normal, as though Proof and Shana had just stepped out to go to lunch.

Then he heard the pounding on the pod next to him. Crap, the others would need rescuing too.

First he opened Grace's pod and then moved to Trina's. He helped both of them out, and they brushed each other off.

"What happened?" asked Trina. "I was in the scullery, crouching behind a stack of pans for the entire snap. It was both boring and horrifying."

"Me too," said Grace. "I was in the command tower, watching the Japanese fighters buzz the tower. It was cool, but I didn't learn anything, really. And I didn't see you."

"I got Little Horn, I think," said William, then he quickly told them the story.

"That's awesome," said Trina.

"But what about Jeremy?" asked Grace.

William looked at Jeremy's pod, which was full of spider-webbed cracks, and thought about it. Their teammate's prostrate body was clearly visible inside. "I mean, he *should* be back to normal. That was the point, after all. Who wants to open it?"

Nobody dared to speak. Finally Grace said, "I'll do it."

Grace went over to the pod and looked down and then looked back at them. "You volunteered," said Trina.

Trina edged her way toward the exit as Grace slowly extended her index finger toward the open button.

"Come on," said William, "don't chicken out. What's the worst that could happen?"

Grace looked at him with sad eyes. "I could release a dangerous ancient entity into our only sanctuary."

"But besides that?"

She didn't answer. Instead, Grace merely pressed the button. The pod cover slid back, revealing Jeremy. He appeared to be back to normal.

"Jeremy? How are you feeling?"

Their teammate sat up, blinked twice, and looked around. "What happened to me? The last I remember, Little Horn was on me in some concentration camp. Then I wake up on a battleship."

"Little Horn happened."

As they undid his cuff and pulled him out, Grace explained the events. When she finished, the four team members looked at each other.

"I guess this is graduation," said Trina, "even though there's nobody here to celebrate it with us."

"Are you sure they're gone?" asked Jeremy.

"They could be in the galley."

"Or in Proof's room."

"Let's have a look," said Grace.

They fanned out through the station, checking the rooms. William had a queasy feeling in his stomach, as though he were looking through a place that he had once lived but had since moved on from.

A scream filled the corridor. It was from Trina, and it came from the direction of Hunter's room.

William and Jeremy and Grace ran down the corridor and crowded in the doorway. Lying on the ground were Shana and Proof, blood staining their shirts and pooling on the ground beneath them. Both had suffered what seemed to be multiple shallow knife wounds. William also saw that they both had defensive injuries too, cuts to the hands.

"Oh my God!" shouted Trina, "are you okay?"

"We're alive," said Proof.

"Who did this?" asked Jeremy.

"It was Hunter," said Shana, as they propped her up against the wall. Trina pulled bedsheets off the mattress to stop Shana's bleeding. Grace did the same for Proof.

"I think it was Little Horn," said Proof, breathing heavily as Grace tended to him. "It was hard to tell the difference. I think they've . . . blended together." He took a breath. "He was trying to kill everyone on the team, but we protected you. We put a temporary lock on the pod tank door that prevented him from getting inside."

"Then you saved our lives," said William.

Proof managed a weak grin. "I need you to do something for me."

"Anything."

"Call the Ancient Engineer."

"How?"

"There's a globe on Shana's desk, a very small one. Just touch it."

William ran down the hall toward Shana's desk. On a corner of it was a small opaque white globe, about the size of an orange. It sat inconspicuously on top of some papers. He hadn't noticed it before. He reached out and touched it, holding his fingers against the surface. The globe glowed bright white. The word *coming* spelled itself on the opaque surface.

"All this time, it was that easy," William said to himself.

By the time he ran back to Hunter's room, the Ancient Engineer had already appeared and was kneeling before Proof and Shana. He wore the same gray wool suit as before. The other three team members were standing flat against the wall, aghast.

"He just materialized in the middle of the room," whispered Jeremy, his face white.

"Right next to me," whispered Trina. "I almost crapped my pants."

Nodding sympathetically, William whispered back, "Yeah, he said he tends to forget that it weirds people out."

The Ancient Engineer was passing his palms over Proof and Shana, who were weak and pale from the blood loss. William glimpsed the same flash of light in the Ancient Engineer's palms that he'd seen while he was in the medical bay. The Ancient Engineer looked up. "Well, their bodies are stabilized, so at least we won't lose these shells. Where should we put them?"

William felt oddly confident around the Ancient Engineer. Their first meeting had done a lot to dispel the nerves. "In the sick bay. There's exactly two beds."

"Then let's carry them there."

They formed two human chairs with their arms. William took the Ancient Engineer's hands, which felt soft but strong, and transported Proof down the hall, still wrapped in a bedsheet. Trina and Grace followed with Shana.

When they'd deposited the two patients in the sick bay and made them comfortable, the Ancient Engineer walked back into the corridor, mopping his brow. The four team members watched him, amazed by his tiniest movements.

He noticed them watching him. "It's true. I sweat just like you."

"In this form, you do," said William.

The Ancient Engineer turned to them. "I request that all of you meet me in the galley. I have to make an announcement."

He disappeared into thin air. Jeremy spun around. "Where did he go?"

"I hate it when he does that," said William.

"What do you think he's going to tell us?" asked Grace.

"Let's find out," said William.

They moved down the hallway toward the galley. Instinctively, each team member reached out for the others' hands. William felt his heart palpitating. He looked at Grace and saw the nervousness in her eyes.

"I'd really prefer not to spend the next millennium cycling

in and out of Menoram," she said. "I want to make a difference."

"Me too. But it's not up to us anymore," said William.

They entered the galley. The Ancient Engineer was already there, seated at the table in the same place he was when William met him a few nights earlier. This time, however, he was looking at a screen, which was propped on the table at an angle that should've been impossible without any visible means of support. His brow was furrowed, and he appeared lost in thought.

The four team members stood in the doorway, uncomfortable, waiting for him to notice them. Finally he looked up.

"So I just ran the numbers, and you made it," he said.

"What did we make?"

"You're all CA3s. Sufficient empathy achieved."

The team members felt their hearts leaping out of their chests. They looked at one another, eyes dancing with happiness. The Ancient Engineer continued: "It was dicey, but the algorithms really liked some of your late moves, particularly yours, William. You didn't need to ask for another tag-along to go back and get Jeremy and fight Little Horn."

"It was the right thing to do," William said.

The Ancient Engineer stood up and came around the table and offered handshake to each of them in turn.

"I'm really shocked," said Grace. "Proof told us that we either made it as a team or we didn't make it at all."

"We lost a member," added Jeremy.

The Ancient Engineer's eyes widened in frustration. "Yes, I'm very aware of *that* situation." He shook his head. "Hunter is something new. I've never seen a CA2 with so much potential go crashing down so quickly and so deliberately."

"Did he have help getting back into the station after he was taken away?" asked Grace.

The Ancient Engineer acknowledged. "I activated the Blaugrad Mechanism, for the first time ever."

"The blue mist?"

He nodded. "Proof hadn't ever seen it either. That's why he was unsure. Truth be told, I wasn't sure it was going to work, but it did. It took him directly to a holding pen. I call it suspended animation, but eventually he had help escaping." He paused for a moment. "To be honest, it was still in beta. I really should've put him somewhere more secure."

"What do you think he's going to do?" asked William.

The Ancient Engineer shrugged. "There've been other rogue agents like him before, but none quite as talented. I'm very concerned that he has already turned against us."

"Ancient Engineer," said Trina, "can I ask, did you make an exception for our team because of him?"

"Yes," he said, taking his seat again behind the screen. "There was absolutely no dealing with Hunter, that much was clear. No negotiating with terrorists, even emotional terrorists. And now that it appears he has joined with Little Horn, well, that is really quite a force to be reckoned with." He looked up, intensity in his eyes. "Your job, your future mission, *all* of you, is to contend with this new entity they've formed."

William cleared his throat. "Can you tell us about that mission?"

The Ancient Engineer casually tapped his screen. "I was just setting it up. Would you like to see your next lives as full-fledged humans?"

"This is not a tag-along?" asked Jeremy.

The Ancient Engineer shook his head. "Nope. You have full lives."

"More than five hundred breaths?" asked William.

"You get *all* of the breaths," replied the Ancient Engineer, grinning. "Millions of them."

"And are we going together?" asked Trina.

"You'll all be on earth at the same time, and that's as much as I can say." He held up a warning finger. "I'm not going to sugarcoat it. This mission is going to be tough, and your deep understanding of eternal matters is going to be tested. But if you learn to surrender yourself to something higher, you have the opportunity to change the world, for the better."

The team let out a spontaneous whoop, eager to learn more about what lay in store for them.

www.ingramcontent.com/pod-product-compliance
Lightning Source LLC
Chambersburg PA
CBHW020406210626
46816CB00006BB/2145

* 9 7 8 0 9 9 9 2 8 8 7 1 9 *